BLACK ROSE

(Obsession Inc. Book 3)

DORI LAVELLE

Black Rose (Obsession Inc. Book 3)
Dori Lavelle
Copyright © 2018
All Rights Reserved.

This book is a work of fiction. Names, characters, places and incidents are products of the author's imagination or are used fictitiously. Any resemblance to actual events or locales or persons, living or dead, is entirely coincidental.

The scanning, uploading and distribution of this book via the internet or any other means without the permission of the publisher is illegal and punishable by law. Please purchase only authorized electronic editions, and do not participate in or encourage electronic piracy of copyrighted materials. Your support of the author's rights is appreciated.

Cover design: Dori Lavelle
Editor: Miss Editrix and Mystique Editing

This is for you.

1

My eyes open an inch at a time. I want to keep them shut. My mind wants to stay awake, to stay alert.

I sit upright, my body feeling as though it has no bones at all. One glance out the window tells me we're in the air, but not for long. I can already feel the sensation of Dax's private plane lowering to the ground.

Barely moving my head, I glance around me. Dax is nowhere to be seen.

Shortly before we left the yacht and he'd forced me onto the plane, I fought him with the little energy I had left, leaving bite marks on his hand.

Unable to handle me, he had given me a shot which put me to sleep immediately.

I'm still his prisoner with no promise of escape. I cannot begin to imagine how to escape from this hell. He's a ruthless murderer. He killed so many without blinking an eye. He killed his own mother. He would not think twice about killing me.

That's the only reason why I sit here, afraid, terrified to even breathe.

My eyes start to close again, my body begs me to give in to sleep. I refuse and wait for him to return. I don't have to wait for long.

His smile is wide as he strides down the aisle, coming to sit next to me. His finger traces the length of my cheekbone. I recoil within.

"Welcome back, baby. You're just in time."

Where's he taking me? Which part of the world is he going to torture me in now?

When I don't respond, he doesn't force me. I turn my head to look back out the window, ignoring him.

"Do you want something to drink?"

"Yes, please." My lips are so dry they're cracking. Not even my saliva can soften them.

There's a risk he could put something in the water to drug me. But I don't feel I have a choice. My thirst is overwhelming.

He hands me a plastic cup. I'm barely able to hold it. I lower it to my lap and look back out the window at the fluffy, white clouds, thinking about what he did to me, to my baby.

I had no idea if I had wanted to keep the baby, but even if I didn't, I would've found the right parents for my child.

My stomach still cramps from the abortion medication he snuck into my body. I'm trying hard to ignore the pain, and the emptiness.

I lift the cup to my lips and take a small sip. As thirsty as I am, it takes me longer to drink the water than it should, but finally, I lick the last drop from my lips, and he takes the cup from me.

"Good girl. You need all your energy. I'll get you something to eat."

He disappears again and returns with a salmon sandwich. I force myself to eat at least half of it. He's right, I do need the strength.

Finally, the plane touches the ground and I sigh with silent relief. I'm terrified of what will come next but being on solid ground is safer than in the air where I have nowhere to run. In fact, it's also safer than being on the Black Mamba yacht, surrounded by the dangers of the sea.

He escorts me to the bathroom and when I'm done, instead of asking me to follow him off the plane, he gathers me into his arms.

He's well aware of how weak I am. He had found pleasure in breaking me, emptying me. Now I'm nothing but a shell, a shadow of the person I once was.

He descends the staircase with me in his arms, waiting to find out what comes next. There's a sound of a tractor in the distance, and those of cows mooing. A wave of panic assails me.

He has brought me to a farm as he promised he would. I try not to think about what tortures await me. Knowing Dax as well as I do, I'm in for a nasty surprise.

Trying not to panic, I remind myself that this is better than it was before. There are more opportunities for me to escape on the ground than on water.

He lowers me onto the passenger seat of a dusty truck and drives down a dirty path leading to a farmhouse.

I don't speak to him and he doesn't strike up a conversation. The only sounds are those of our heavy breathing.

When we arrive at our destination, he opens my door and lifts me from the vehicle, then approaches the farmhouse I had seen from a distance. Some chickens run past us and dust swirls upward from the ground. I close my eyes as it enters them, wishing I could escape this moment.

It's not over. I'm not ready to give up. As soon as I get my strength back, I'll come up with a plan to get away from the monster.

The front door creaks as he pushes it open with a shoulder. The moment he steps inside, stale, musty air fills my lungs. The house smells like no one has lived in it for quite some time.

"Home sweet home." He kisses me on the cheek.

He doesn't seem to mind that I don't

answer as he lowers me onto a flowery couch that smells old. Above me, the ceiling is stained and dirty.

Hands in his pockets, his gaze sweeps the room. "There's a lot that needs to be done around here," he says. "But we will make this into a beautiful home. You'll never want to leave again. Not that you can anyway." He returns his gaze to me. "You won't get past the electric fence surrounding the property."

A flash of wild grief tears through me. Of course he has strong measures in place to keep me trapped here. This is my new prison. He will not make it easy for me to get away again. This time, if I try and fail, I have no doubt I'll end up dead. He will kill me like he killed his mother and his employees.

"I could have paid someone to renovate the farmhouse for us, but I figured it would be romantic to make it our own together, don't you think?"

He waits for an answer that won't come. Instead of responding, I curl up on the dingy couch, my hands between my knees, my back turned away from him. I close my eyes, the only way I can shut him out.

Any moment now, he could strike. He hates nothing more than being ignored.

In my darkness, I imagine myself back home with my sister, holding on to her. Maybe if I focus hard enough on what I want, it would come true. Since my body is helpless at the moment, I only have my mind to rely on.

"Do you want something more to eat?" His question lands on deaf ears.

I wish he would go and rot in hell. I can't even bear to be in the same room as him. Even though he believes we're married, I hope we will share different bedrooms like we did on the Black Mamba. The mere thought of sleeping next to him night after night causes ice to spread through my stomach.

He makes me sick and I cannot wait for him to suffer the consequences of his actions. I have never hated anyone as much as I hate Dax Pierce. One day he will not only pay for what he did to me, but also to the innocent women who came before me.

He repeats his question, but my eyes

remain closed. Finally, he relents and sits in an armchair next to the couch. He watches me in silence.

Although the air is thick with his anger and frustration, he doesn't say a word. Tense silence hovers between us and I count the seconds before he explodes. I know he will eventually. It's only a matter of time.

It was not my intention to fall asleep, but the next time I open my eyes, the sky outside the window is blushing. How long have I been asleep for? Had he spiked the water he had given me on the plane or were remnants of the drug he had used earlier still coursing through my veins?

Panic blossoms inside my chest. I hate that the sun is setting. Dax is a man of the darkness. Most of his cruelties happen at night. Maybe he thinks the night will cover his evil acts.

I comfort myself with the thought that he will not try to sleep with me this time since the bleeding from the forced abortion has not yet ceased.

This time I sit up on the couch. When he serves me an avocado chicken salad, I think of pushing it away, but I can't afford not to eat. My stomach is already complaining.

He waits patiently for me to finish my dinner, then he locks the doors and windows. Each window I can see from the couch has a heavy lock. Finished, he lowers himself onto the couch opposite mine.

"We'll sleep in here tonight. I'll take this couch so you have enough space. I'll show you the rest of the house tomorrow. The rooms are a mess." He blows me a kiss. "Goodnight, darling."

I let out a silent sigh of relief and lay myself down again, resting my head on my hands.

The sky outside the window darkens and I'm still awake, forcing my mind to come up with an escape plan.

Dax is not sleeping either. I don't need to look at him to know his eyes are on me. What's going on through his sick mind? Is he really proud of everything he has done? Is he thinking of new ways to up his game?

In the darkness, the tears squeeze through the corners of my eyes. I do my best to stop my shoulders from shaking and press my lips together so I don't make a sound. I don't know if I'll ever forgive myself for giving Dax entry into my life. I should have listened to Curtis's warnings about him. I should have chosen Curtis, whose love was real unlike Dax's fucked-up version.

"I know you're upset," he says in the dark.

My heart stutters at the sound of his voice and my crying comes to a screeching halt.

"Everything will be okay again. I promise you that. I'll make you happy again."

His words repeat in my mind, over and over again, until I fall drowsy and tumble into the arms of sleep where more nightmares await me.

2

I wake up to the sound of a rooster crowing and chickens clucking outside the window. Shit, I'm still here and it's morning. Another day to spend with the devil.

My movements are slow as I turn to face the other side. I groan at the discomfort brought on by lying on one side for hours. But no amount of pain can compare to the inner ache pulsing inside my heart. I dreamed of my baby, a little girl I didn't get a chance to hold as she was taken away from me as soon as she was born.

Even fast asleep, I'd felt the pain of loss that still plagues me, and guilt that I did not do enough to protect her.

"Ready to start the day?" He plants his

hands on his knees.

The only response he gets is a groan as I stretch my aching legs. The bones in my body feel as though they're fractured in some places.

My stomach clenches when he gets up and comes to my couch. He grabs my hands a little too tight and pulls me to a sitting position. As soon as he lets go, I lay myself down again. I don't have the physical or the mental strength to even sit. My rage sears the inside of my chest before spreading to my entire body. There will be a high price to pay for this, but frankly, right now I don't have the strength to care.

He rests a warm hand on my cheek. "I know this doesn't look like a fairytale, but it can be. We'll create it together. But you have to work with me here."

"I'm tired." My lips barely move as I speak.

"Then you have to eat something. I'll make you breakfast. Let me take care of you."

He runs a hand over my bald head. My skin crawls at his touch. I don't move away, though. I'm already walking on dangerous ground. My inner bravery does not make me less afraid of the monster that lurks behind his eyes, waiting to attack when it doesn't get what it wants.

His eyes seem darker today, always a sign that he's annoyed. I've had enough time to study him, to know when I've gone too far with my rebellion.

I grit my teeth and force myself to sit. Everything around this living room looks filthy with stained carpet, dust and cobwebs everywhere. This new environment is a far cry from the luxury we left behind on the Black Mamba.

This time, I allow him to pull me to my feet, to take me to a bathroom that's as dirty as the rest of the house. It has a dirty bath and a shower cubicle with a molded curtain hanging at the entrance, a stained sink, and peeling yellow paint on the walls.

A tiny window is positioned above the bath. Like all the other windows, it also has a lock in it. Dax may not have done anything to make this place livable, but he invested a lot of work in making sure it's a solid prison. Hindering my escape was his priority.

When his fingers reach for a strap of my silky nightdress from the yacht, my body tenses up and I take a step back. "Don't."

"It's all right, sweetheart. I won't hurt you." He draws me back to him and sweeps the strap off my shoulder. "You need a shower, that's all. Let me help you."

A shower sounds tempting. It's been a while since I had one, but I'm cringing at the idea of him washing me. What if the act turns him on?

The worry is still on my mind, but I step into the shower and under the warm jet of water. The soothing water on my skin feels so good I even forget the grime at my feet.

Ignoring the danger close by, I close my eyes and give the water permission to wash over me, to follow the curves of my body, to drip into my eyes and mouth. I even swallow some of it to quench the thirst that has returned.

Dax hands me a sponge and a bottle of shower gel. The stuff he gives me looks new. He must have done a lot of shopping and stocked up before we arrived on the farm. Among the dirt on the sink I noticed a cosmetic bag filled with toothbrushes—

toothpaste, lotions, shower gels, tampons, pads, and several other toiletries.

My worries melt away when he doesn't join me in the shower or offer to wash me himself.

I take my time scrubbing my body. It sickens me to shower with him watching me, but the water is the best comfort I've had in a while and I don't want to get out. As water trickles to my feet, I try not to glance down, afraid of what I'd see. But my eyes are drawn like a magnet to the little smear of blood disappearing into the drain, washed away but still visible in my mind's eye. The blood is not much, not anymore, but it's enough to make my raw wounds ache. It reminds me of the baby I'll never have. It warns me of how dangerous Dax is.

Finally, Dax reaches into the shower and turns off the tap. He hands me a towel, a fresh pair of underwear, a pad, and my filthy nightdress.

"I'll wait outside for you," he says and leaves the bathroom. He doesn't close the door.

Alone for a few minutes, I dress and use

the toilet. I'm surprised there's not much blood left. I'm sure it will stop entirely in the next few days. But how many days would I be stuck on this farm with this monster? How many days until someone rescues me, or I find a way out before he kills me? I hope I won't find out when it's too late.

Once I'm done, he comes back inside and takes me by the hand. He leads me through the bedroom adjoining the bathroom, down the dark hallway, and into the kitchen.

It's the first time I'm seeing it because last night we ate dinner in the living room. It looks worse than what I've seen in the rest of the house so far.

In the middle of a dusty kitchen table is a red bucket with a white rag hanging on the side, filled with soapy water.

The stove has food dried up on it. Something must have boiled over. The sink is overflowing with dirty dishes that give off a rotten smell. My stomach churns. This whole place is a breeding ground for bacteria. It will take hours and a lot of energy to scrub this place clean.

I'm surprised Dax doesn't react to the dirt in the house. He's walking around with a smirk on his face as though everything is working out as he's planned. I guess it is.

"Don't worry about the dirt," he says. "Unfortunately the previous owner was a pig." He turns a knob on the stove. "This stove and most of the stuff around here doesn't even work, but we don't need any of it." He turns to me, his face happy and relaxed. "I hope you won't mind cooking our food over an open fire until I get us a new stove."

My eyes widen. He must be out of his damn mind. I want to tell him as much, but I hold myself back. This is not the right time. I can't fight him yet.

He lifts a grocery bag from the floor and lifts out a brand new kettle. "After breakfast, you can start with the cleaning."

While he's busy fiddling with the kettle, his back turned to me, I take some steps back until my back meets the edge of the sink. My eyes are focused on the dirty pot within my arm's reach.

Before I can do anything, he moves to the fridge and yanks it open.

It's packed with so much food that he can't seem to decide what to take out. I take his moment of indecision to act.

My hands move fast toward the pot and close around the handle. I don't waste time thinking about the possible consequences of what I'm about to do. My fingers tighten around the handle and I send the pot flying through the air headed for his head. But he turns around in time and ducks.

Shocked, just as I am, by the sudden turn of events, he sways from side to side. He pulls himself together faster than I can recover. He backhand slaps me so hard across the face that I crumple to the floor, unprepared for the blow. My body tenses up as it waits for him to kick me while I'm down, or to kill me.

To be honest, right now death doesn't seem like such a bad idea. I reject the idea immediately. I can't leave Christa behind. She needs me. I need to survive this torture for her sake.

Checking out of life is out of the question. Especially since my death would also mean he wins. Dax can't get away with this. He cannot live to kill another day. I have to keep fighting him.

He hovers over me, feet planted on both sides of my body, his face like thunder. His mouth is working as though he wants to say something but can't find the right words. It must be a shock to him to realize he has not broken me completely.

He's in for many more surprises. He has no idea that I'm just getting started.

"It's only you and me now," he says, glancing out the window. "If I kill you, no one will know. If I strangle you right now, you would be my dirty little secret. You don't want that, do you?"

I raise my burning eyes to his face, unable to hide my disgust and hatred for him.

He doesn't seem to care. He simply walks away to fill the kettle and plug it in. While I'm still on the dirty floor, he makes himself a cup of coffee and a sandwich. He doesn't offer me any.

Once he's done with his breakfast, he brushes the crumbs to the floor, and returns to me. "Your punishment will be to clean this house until there's no speck of dust left in sight."

He lifts the bucket from the table and dumps it next to me, water splashing from it. Then he yanks me to my feet and I don't resist.

My cheeks burn with humiliation as I gaze into the water. He's treating me like a slave, as he had done to his mother.

"You know by now I can do much worse than this." He crosses his arms in front of his chest. "Don't push me."

He grabs the rag and pushes it into my hand. I refuse to hold on to it.

"Don't be a bitch. You know what I do to women who disobey me." He grips my hand and curls my fingers around the rag by force.

That's it then. The monster is back. If I want to live, I need to obey, for now.

I dip the rag into the water and scrub every surface in the kitchen. It takes me back to when I was a cleaning lady at the Baroque Hotel, but the work is so much harder when you're forced to do it.

While he drinks more coffee with a thunderous expression on his face, I scrub the counter, the table, the stove, and the windows. The only time he speaks is to tell me when I've missed a spot.

By the time I'm done with the kitchen, it looks transformed. The dust is gone, the majority of the dirt has disappeared down the drain, and the air seems a little bit clearer.

After I sweep and wipe the floor, he drags me to several more rooms, and finally to the living room for more cleaning. I'm exhausted out of my mind, so much that I don't even resist.

He lowers himself onto the couch and continues to watch me acting as his personal maid. At one point I turn to find him sitting with his legs apart, his dick free and his hands gliding up and down the length. I look away again because the sight disgusts me. How can this possibly turn him on? I keep my back turned from him even when he finally grunts. I only turn at the sound of his zipper.

My head is swimming now after so much work and nothing to eat. I sway toward a stand shelf to continue my work, but the moment I arrive, whatever little energy I have left drains from my body.

More sweat pops out of my skin and black dots appear before my eyes.

I sink to the floor fast. He gets to me before I can reach it. I'm surprised when he picks me up and takes me to the couch, which is less disgusting after I had beaten the dust out of it earlier.

"That's enough for today. It's getting late anyway. You'll continue tomorrow." His voice sounds like it's coming from a distance away.

As my eyes fall shut on their own, I'm terrified of what tomorrow will bring.

3

Dax shakes me awake before dawn.

"You've slept long enough. It's time to get back to work." The chill in his voice cools my spine and drives me to obey.

I'm so hungry that when he gives me two slices of plain bread and water to wash the food down with—before I start cleaning—I mumble a sincere thank you.

When I'm done eating, I don't fight him or wait for him to tell me to get started. I rise from the table to clean it up, and wash up.

"It didn't have to be like this, you know." He lifts a Granny Smith to his lips. "But I have to punish you for constantly throwing my kindness and generosity back in my face. I gave you everything, Emma, in LA and on the Yacht. I showered you with every luxury imaginable." He bites into the apple and says nothing more as he chews. He continues after he swallows. "Now you have to get used to this kind of life. But you're still more fortunate than most."

I wash the dirty dishes in silence and he no longer speaks. He also doesn't leave me alone. I keep wishing I would come across a fork or knife I could use as a weapon, but there is nothing.

When I'm done washing up, I face him, fingers crossed behind my back. "Where do you want me to clean today?" Maybe being his maid is not such a bad idea.

Keeping busy keeps him from doing other terrible things to me.

"Aren't you going to respond to what I said to you? Didn't you hear me?" His tone is tinged with annoyance.

"I heard you fine." My upper lip curls with disgust.

He rubs his brow as though to chase off a headache. "And what do you have to say?"

"I'm sorry that I did not appreciate the

things you offered me." I try hard to keep my tone from being sharp even though flames of anger are shooting through me. I have to pull it together. I have to be careful. Pissing him off doesn't serve me at this point.

A quick glance out the window reminds me of how huge the property is. It would be hard for me to run without him catching up. From where I'm standing, I can't even see the fence that's waiting to electrify me. It would be hard to get away without a car.

"Good." His smirk returns. "I want you to clean our bedroom. We'll be sleeping there tonight."

With him behind me, chewing on another apple, he leads me to the master bathroom where I took a shower yesterday.

The room is spacious, but messy and dirty, with torn curtains, a stained mattress, broken furniture, and dust everywhere. A picture frame with a faded picture hangs askew on the wall above the bed.

A sneeze tickles the back of my nose and I let it out. It's a wonder I have not sneezed non-stop since entering this house.

I don't even know where to start. I look around me, my hands already numb with exhaustion from the cleaning I've already done. Even the bones in my hands are aching. But I have no choice. I have to work so he doesn't find an excuse to hurt me.

I move to one of the windows to open it so the stale air escapes the room, but it's locked.

"Let me," he says from behind me. I step aside. I watch him pull a set of keys from his pocket.

As soon as all the windows are thrown open, the sounds of animals enter--cows, sheep, goats, horses.

As a kid I always thought a farm is the true definition of freedom. I loved spending time on the farm belonging to a friend of our father's, running around an open field, taking care of animals, and milking cows. I was always disappointed whenever our visits came to an end. Who would have thought I would one day be trapped on a farm with a mad man.

I start with the windows, to make the room less claustrophobic. The grime on the edges takes so much time to scrub away. I really don't get why he bought a dirty place. Did he know from the beginning that he would use the cleaning as punishment? Whatever the case, he succeeded.

He's sitting on a plastic chair by the door, gazing down at his phone and occasionally in my direction.

By the time I'm done with the windows, my back is aching and sweat is trickling down my temples. I don't have enough energy for this. My body aches to sit, but I don't dare to take a break while he watches my every move.

I move on to the bed and touch the dirty mattress. My stomach roils at the sight of the stains. Will I end up sleeping on this thing?

I look up at him. "Should I . . . should I wash it?" I'll be doing it more for me than him.

"No need. I have a new mattress in the basement. We're not sleeping on someone else's piss and God-knows-what."

"Okay." My posture slumps with relief. Ignoring the mattress, I clean the wooden headboard and nightstands.

"Sorry for the inconvenience, my love. I'm afraid the previous owner didn't have time to clean up since I wanted the farm immediately. No one has lived here for years. I'm sorry you have to clean up their mess."

He's talking as if he really cares when we both know he's enjoying my misery. He jerked off to me cleaning, for God's sake. That's how much he enjoys watching me suffer. What an asshole.

I scrub everything to a shine, I even remove the hanging picture from the wall and clean the wallpaper.

When I dust off the radio inside the cupboard of one of the nightstands, I make a mental note to find a way to see if it works. Maybe at some point he will get tired of watching me every second and I'd grab my chance. It would be nice to hear news from the outside world, to hear someone else's voice.

Before I move on to the bathroom, he tells me to take a break, giving me a glass of water which I accept gratefully. My hands shake as I bring it to my lips.

When I'm done drinking, he asks me to follow him to the basement to help him bring up the new mattress and bed sheets. The mattress is heavy. I drop it several times and almost get crushed by its weight, but eventually we manage to bring it into the room and drop it onto the bed.

A few minutes later, the pristine white sheets and pillows completely transform and brighten up the room. The bed looks so inviting, I'm dying to throw myself onto it and fall asleep.

I don't remember ever being this tired in my whole life. I've never cleaned until my hands are raw, not even at the Baroque Hotel. I'm so overcome with exhaustion that even standing is hard for me, making me feel dizzy. I want to obey him, but my body can't take it anymore. It forces me into a nearby armchair while my terrified eyes are fixed on Dax's face. He will punish me for this.

"What do you think you're doing?" he growls. "Get the fuck up. You have a lot of work to do before cooking lunch."

I push myself back to my feet, my teeth gritted. I wish I could wrap my hands around his neck and strangle him. He should try doing the work I did on little food and drink.

"Clean the floor," he orders.

As he continues to watch from the doorway, I get to my knees and sink the rag into the water.

I scrub the floor until my eyes fill with tears of exhaustion. By the time I'm done and back on my feet, I can barely stand. I'm swaying from side to side, on the verge of sinking to the floor like I did yesterday.

"Hang in there, my baby." He appears in front of me with open arms. "You did a fantastic job." He pulls me into his arms and holds me for a while. I lean into him because I'm finding it hard to carry my own weight.

He finally pulls back. "Let's go to the kitchen." He takes my hand and leads me out of the room and into the kitchen, where he sits me down at the table and pours me a cup of orange juice. The juice tastes like heaven on my tongue.

"I love you. I'm also really proud of you.

I love your dedication toward making our new home beautiful for us. We will be so happy here, you'll see." His fingers brush the back of my neck. "We are enough, just you and me. We don't need any damn kids to ruin everything."

I bite my tongue to prevent myself from lashing out at him. My hands tighten around the cup so hard I'm glad it's not glass, or it would have shattered.

"What do you want for lunch?" he asks, moving to the fridge. He places all kinds of sandwich ingredients in front of me. I guess he told the truth when he said the stove does not work. That's why we're living on sandwiches and cold food.

When I don't answer, he prepares a peanut butter sandwich and drops it in front of me on the table, not bothering to put it on a plate. "You need to keep your strength up. Finish it."

He doesn't need to beg me to eat because I relish every crumb. The entire time I'm eating my food, I'm gazing out the window, wishing for my freedom, so many questions running through my mind.

I'm so deep in my thoughts that I jump

at the sound of a sudden loud noise. I return to the present to find Dax glaring at me, his fist on the table in front of me. He must have slammed it against the surface.

"Stop doing that." His voice is loaded. "You have to stop ignoring me when I speak to you."

"What. . . what did you say?" I swallow the bread in my mouth.

"I was telling you what your next task is, but you just sat there ignoring me like a fool."

"I'm sorry. I was far away."

"Well, stop that shit. I want you back here with me. This is where you belong now." He brings his face close to mine. I can feel his hot breath on my face. "Stop wishing you were someplace else."

I meet his eyes without flinching. "Where do you want me to clean next?"

He blows out a frustrated breath. "You will sweep outside. There's chicken shit all over the place."

"Fine." I lift myself from the chair. Now that I've eaten, I'm stronger than I felt before. Bring it on.

Outside, he hands me a rake and I get

started on cleaning away the shit while the chickens run around, replacing what I cleaned away with fresh new droppings.

Dust rises from the ground and into my eyes. It makes me sneeze, but I don't mind it much. It's like a protective cloak. I wish it could cover me completely and make me disappear.

I want all this to be over. I want to fall to the ground and stay there. I'm suddenly tired again. My body aches for a break, but he's watching. I keep going.

Once I'm done, he tells me he'll set up an outdoor kitchen in the area I just cleared. I don't bother to ask how he intends on doing that. I continue cleaning the place, picking all kinds of trash from the ground, dumping it into a nearby bin.

"We'll enjoy a warm meal tonight." He points at a dirty piece of paper that I failed to pick up. He waits for me to pick it up before he continues. "I'm sure you're ready to eat a proper meal. It's time we start living like normal people."

"Yes," I mumble. I'm not in a position to pretend I don't want to eat. It won't be a good idea to give him a reason to starve or beat me.

I must be doing something right because when I'm done, he tells me I can go and take a nap.

Rest is exactly what I need, but I'm unable to relax when he decides he needs a nap too and lies next to me.

When I turn my back to him, he wraps an arm around my waist. My body stiffens. It's hard to ignore the touch of his dick against my back.

It's only a matter of time before he insists that I have sex with him, to fulfil his sick desires.

I close my eyes and visualize things the way I would want them to be, what I want to happen.

My body relaxes when he doesn't make a move to fuck me. I'm starting to drift off when he speaks.

"You've made me wait long enough. Soon you'll have to carry out your duties as a wife. You will make love to your husband."

I stiffen, but before I can panic, I tell myself that *soon* doesn't have to be today. It doesn't have to be tomorrow either. Right now I have to focus on getting back as much of my strength as I possibly can. I will worry about the rest later.

The thought that one day he will pay a high price for his crimes lulls me to sleep.

4

Dax wakes me when the sun is about to sink into the horizon.

My sleep had been so deep that I'm momentarily disoriented. This time my slumber was a great escape with no nightmares to disturb it.

I sit up and rub the blurriness from my eyes.

"Let's get dinner started, sleepy head. I'm glad you got some much-needed rest." He takes my hand and leads me out of the bedroom as though we're a couple in love.

He takes me back to the clearing outside the kitchen. Dax had been serious about turning it into a kitchen. Three stones stand opposite each other in the middle of the space, a shiny pot balanced on top of them.

He brings out two chairs and asks me to sit. His voice is gentler than it had been earlier today.

"Since you did such a great job today, I'll take care of dinner tonight. I'm thinking potato and meat stew." He scratches his beard. "But I have to do something first. Get up for a moment."

I do as I'm told, and watch perplexed as he places the chair next to the pole of a clothesline. He comes back to take my hand and sits me down again. To my horror, he reaches into his back pocket and removes handcuffs. "This is a precaution. I'll be going in and out of the kitchen and I can't afford for you to do anything stupid."

I try to stop him from handcuffing me, but he's stronger and he does the job with so much speed I'm almost shocked when the handcuffs click around my wrist.

The truth is, I don't blame him for feeling the need to handcuff me. He knows that if I find an opportunity to escape, I'll do it.

He disappears into the kitchen several

times to get food and everything else that he needs. Then he bends over the stones and pulls out a match. It takes him a while to get the fire going, but once it does, he straightens to his full height, pleased with himself.

He comes to give me a kiss on the lips and tips my head back to look into my eyes, which are tearing up from the smoke.

"This is how some villagers do it in Africa, cooking over an open fire. The food actually tastes so much better." He's looking at me, but he has a faraway expression on his face now. "I should take you to Africa one day. You will love it." He steps away from me but doesn't stop talking.

My attention has drifted from him. I'm distracted by the sounds of the chickens scratching the ground. I cannot see them, but they have to be nearby, in their coop perhaps.

"It's so peaceful out here." He tilts his head back and looks up at the dark sky. "Who needs the city?" He goes on and on, but I'm grateful that this time he doesn't demand answers from me. He's completely lost in the perfect world he has built for himself.

My stomach rumbles when the meat finally releases its delicious aromas. It feels like hours until he finishes cooking and comes to me with a steaming bowl. Instead of removing the handcuffs, he feeds me himself. I eat up every bite he offers me. The food is not nearly enough, but I'm afraid to ask for more.

My mouth is still watering when he brings his own chair next to mine and sits to eat his own food, while telling me more stories about Africa, especially how he had enjoyed spending a few weeks in an Angolan village.

"I also met some stunning women over there." His voice trails off. "One in particular caught my attention. She was a beauty, but she turned out to be a whore. Like all the rest, she betrayed me. And she paid a high price."

"You—"

"Yes, I did. I drowned her in the village lake." He pulls in a breath. "I don't handle betrayal well. You know that, right?"

Chilled by his confession, I nod.

"Great." He gets up without offering me any more food. "Time to move on." He removes the handcuff bracelet from the pole but doesn't open the one around my wrist. He holds my hand as we enter the house. "There's something special I want you to see. A special room just for you."

During the walk down the hallway, my stomach clenches tighter, the food I ate earlier souring. I'm still haunted by what he told me about the woman he killed in Africa, and I dread to think about what he has in store for me. His surprises are never pleasant.

He brings me to a halt in front of a closed door. "Ready?" He doesn't wait for an answer. He unlocks the door and swings it open.

I stand in the doorway looking into a pitch-black room. It must not have any windows. I hope he won't ask me to enter.

"It's okay," he says into my ear. "You can go in." He plants a hand on the middle of my back and leads me inside. Bright light replaces the darkness.

At the sight before me, I let out a scream. I try to run back out, but he grabs me and shuts the door.

"What's wrong?" He smiles. "Don't ruin the fun. I've spent so much time and money preparing this room for you. I couldn't wait for you to see it."

I'm jumping from foot to foot, the hairs at the nape of my neck rising as I gaze down at the floor. It's made completely of glass with snakes of all shapes and sizes slithering underneath it. I knew I wouldn't like his surprise, but never in a million years had I expected this. Being barefoot makes the nasty experience so much worse. It feels as though the snakes are actually touching the soles of my feet.

"Please, get me out of here." I curl my clammy hands into a fist, trying my best to hold it together. But I'm too terrified of snakes to keep calm.

I run to the door again, but he grabs me by the arm and pushes me close to the center of the room. I lose my balance and fall to the floor. I barely touch the glass before he yanks me back to my feet.

"You're not going anywhere." He pushes his hands into his pockets and studies the floor. "These are our babies.

They're some of the deadliest snakes in the world. Some are actually illegal to own in this country." He shrugs. "But no one stops me from getting what I want."

I try to stand on tiptoes, so my entire feet don't touch the floor, but I can't find my balance.

"Don't worry," he says. "They won't harm you. Not unless the glass is broken."

A large yellow snake slithers to where I'm standing. In reaction, my stomach contracts and saliva fills my mouth. Bile follows in such a rush that I'm unable to hold it back. It explodes from me before I can stop it.

"You have to clean that mess up," he says and comes to wipe my mouth with my nightdress. "As I was saying, anyone in this room is safe as long as the glass is intact."

He points to the door. "Outside is a switch. Once I push it, a part of the floor will slide away creating an opening for the snakes to get out. One bite from one of them can be deadly." He comes to me, holds my shaking body tight in his arms. "When you misbehave, I'll bring you here to spend a little time with our babies. Is that what you want?"

"No," I say quickly. Tears flood my eyes. "Please, let me out."

He lets me go and my gaze drops to the floor again. The snakes don't even need to touch me. The sight of them is enough to terrify me.

"Snakes are actually beautiful creatures. They only attack when they feel threatened. As long as they're under there, you're safe. Don't make me change that. Don't forget that we're alone here, and I have the right to end your life if I choose." With those words of warning, he finally takes me out of the room. But not for long.

He brings me back a few minutes later with a bucket of water.

He points to my vomit. "Clean that up."

It's pure torture to clean the floor as it brings me so close to the snakes. I've never cleaned anything so fast in my life. I almost cry out with relief when we're outside again.

I'm still panting with fear when he takes me to the bedroom and gives me something else to wear, a black, shapeless dress that must have belonged to someone who lived here. To me, it's perfect as it covers my body well. Next, he removes my handcuffs and massages my wrists. The discomfort remains.

"I love you, Emma. All the things I did wouldn't have happened if you believed that. You make it so hard to love you sometimes. But I won't stop. I know deep down in your heart, you love me just as much."

I want to burst his bubble, to remind him that my love for him is dead. But an image of the snakes comes to mind and stops me in my tracks.

"I want you to say it." He continues to massage my wrist "Tell me you love me, baby."

If I don't want to be thrown into the dungeon, I have to say it. I have to lie. "I. . . I love you," I say in a shrill voice.

"Say, I love you, Dax."

"I love you, Dax." The words tremble out of my mouth, breaking through my lips. If he's too blind to see I'm lying, it's his own damn fault.

"Good." He lays me down on the bed

and rests a hand on my cheek, makes me look at him. "I'm sorry about all the hard work. After tomorrow, everything will be different, okay? I'm getting you someone to help you out."

"Someone?" I didn't mean to say the word out loud.

"A maid." His face brightens. "You'll have your own personal maid. It's my gift to you. That's how much I love you."

Even though it's a relief to be getting help, I'm terrified for the person who's coming to work for him. On the other hand, maybe it's someone I can work with, someone who might help me escape. Hopefully, I won't be getting another person like Otto.

Since Dax still doesn't try to make love to me, I close my eyes. Tonight, I dream of myself in Curtis's arms.

5

I open my eyes to the choppy sound of a plane in flight. Bitter memories from the Black Mamba flood my mind and my entire body locks with tension. After a few calming breaths, I find the courage to look at my worst nightmare.

He's standing by the window, his back straight as he gazes out. Perhaps sensing I'm watching him, he turns around slowly. The smile on his face is the kind he pastes on when he's about to inflict more pain.

His beige t-shirt is rumpled, his hair and beard unkempt, but his amber eyes are glowing. Every nerve in my body tells me I don't want to know what he has in store for me today.

"Today will be unforgettable." He rushes to the bed and kisses me hard on the lips. "You know how I love surprising you."

His words send shivers of fear down my spine.

I can't find anything to say as I watch him bouncing around the room, unable to contain his excitement. He visibly vibrates with energy. "I should go. Your surprise has arrived." He comes to handcuff me to the bed. "I'll be back. Don't go anywhere."

He's full of shit. Where would I go handcuffed to the bed?

He crosses the room to get to the door. Once there, he turns to blow me a kiss. "You'll love it. I promise."

When he's gone, I try to force my hand out of the handcuff, but of course, I don't have a chance against the steel closed tightly around my wrist.

Just as I'm making myself comfortable in the bed, Dax returns again to lock the windows, even though there's no chance I could get through the bars.

He blows me another kiss and disappears, but I can still feel his presence in the room, so thick as if he were still there.

The sound of his footsteps fades as he makes his way down the hallway. A door, I guess the front door, slams soon after.

When I hear the truck roaring to life, air explodes from my lungs in a gasp.

Blocking my mind from thinking about what surprise he has for me, I try again to pull my hand out of the handcuffs. I know it's a losing game, but that doesn't stop me. After a few tries, I quit because it hurts too much.

I let out a bitter laugh. I'm as paranoid as he is. Even if I were not handcuffed to the bed, I'm not going anywhere anytime soon. I'm chained to him in more ways than one and it terrifies the hell out of me.

I blow out a breath and force my hands to stay still. They're shaking so hard, the handcuffs rattle against the wood.

It's okay, Emma. You will be fine. This is not how your story will end.

I say the words to myself over and over again, until I feel like a broken record. Maybe if I say it often enough, it will turn out to be true. I don't even want to consider the alternative.

It *will* be okay one way or the other. There are two options. Either I'll be dead and unable to hurt anymore, or I'll find a way out.

The longer Dax is away, the more nervous I become, sweat pouring down my temples.

I'm sitting on the edge of the bed now, my right arm pulled towards the headboard and my feet tapping the wooden floor impatiently. I'm not ready for whatever he wants to surprise me with, but not knowing is just as terrifying, if not more so.

Finally, my ears catch the rumble of the truck drawing closer to the house. My pulse starts to race. My toes curl to grip the floor tighter as if it can save me, as if anything or anyone can save me. I wish I could escape this moment, just disappear into thin air like in the fairytales my mother used to read to us when we were kids.

I would have loved to see the look on his face if he were to enter the room and find me gone. But that will never happen. I'll be right here where he left me.

My ears strain to listen to the sound of the front door opening and closing, the sound of his voice, the thud of his footsteps. It's hard to hear much through the rush of fear in my ears. But I catch the noise made by a chair scraping the floor. I know it's coming from the kitchen.

After what feels like forever, he shows up in the room, looking as smug as he had been earlier. "Did you miss me?" He pulls a long, red cloth from his pocket. "I sure *did* miss you. A few minutes away from you feel like an eternity." He grabs the ends of the cloth and pulls it straight with a snap. "It's time for you to meet your surprise." He comes to sit next to me.

"What are you doing?" I ask, trying to stop him from tying the cloth around my eyes.

I swallow hard when he slides it around my neck instead. "Would you rather I tie it here?" He forms a quick knot behind my neck and pulls.

"No," I cry out and he releases immediately. Tears of relief spring to my eyes. I don't try to stop him again.

"Hey, you don't have to be afraid," he

says. "I want to surprise you, that's all. It will all be worth it, trust me."

When he's done blindfolding me, he removes the handcuffs, but only for him to bring both my hands in front of me. He cuffs both wrists together. "You look so sexy with handcuffs on."

On shaky legs, I allow him to guide me out of the room, his arm around my shoulders.

A few awkward steps later, he pulls me to a stop. The door creaks as he opens it. He nudges me forward.

I freeze when I hear labored breathing and moaning. My nerves tense up.

"Are you ready for your surprise?" There's a trace of laughter in his voice.

I nod, knowing that's what he expects. The beads of sweat on my forehead are proof that I'm not ready.

He pulls me to his body, holds me in place, and removes the blindfold.

When I recognize the woman in front of me, blood drains from my face. "No," I say in a strangled voice. "Oh God, not Christa." My hands curl up into fists. "Not my sister."

"See," he says, holding me tight so I don't faint. He brings his mouth to my ear. "I told you this will be the best surprise ever."

This is the most disgusting surprise he has ever given me.

The sight of my sister makes me sick. In addition to being blindfolded, with a piece of cloth that looks exactly like the one that had been around my eyes, her mouth is taped shut. Her head is moving from side to side as she tries but fails to remove the gray tape from her lips.

What's even more humiliating is what she's wearing. Aside from one of the aprons she used to wear in the kitchen of the Baroque Hotel and Spa, she's completely naked. The sides of her breasts spill from the sides of the apron. I can't even imagine how humiliated she feels right now.

As though I also have tape around my mouth, I'm speechless. But I try to speak until I succeed. "Don't, Dax." My wet eyes plead with him not to hurt her. I can't allow my sister to suffer the same fate I've been dealt. He can't kill us both.

"Don't what?" Dax lets me go and goes to remove the blindfold from Christa's eyes.

Her wild, terrified eyes are red and puffy, black mascara smeared around them.

Before I can stop myself, I rush to her side, my knees hitting the floor at her feet. Dax gets to me before I can make contact with her. He yanks me to my feet so fast my blood rushes to my head. "Don't touch her," he warns, his mouth pressed to my ear. "She's only here to be your maid. I won't approve of my wife mingling with the servants."

I scream then, throwing curses at him as I struggle for him to let me go. "Fuck you. She's my sister."

"Not anymore." He tightens his grip around me and presses his hand to my mouth, shutting me up. "You should be thankful she's still alive. I could've asked one of my people to kill her. Would you have preferred her as a corpse?"

When I still don't quit fighting him, he grabs the back of my neck and sends me crashing into the kitchen table, a few inches from where Christa is seated. The edge of the table knocks the air from my lungs. I fall to the ground in a heap, whimpering.

Christa is struggling, trying to free herself, but her hands are handcuffed around the back of the chair.

Tears rolling down my cheeks, I turn to look up into his eyes "I'm begging you. Please, don't hurt her. Let her go. I don't. . . I don't need a maid."

"Bullshit. Have you seen your hands? After all the work you did, they look like crap. You need help and I'm giving it to you."

"Get me someone else. Anyone."

"That's not going to happen." He goes to the fridge and pours himself a glass of water, which he drains in one gulp.

My frantic gaze moves back to Christa. Her head is resting on her shoulder now. Her hair is bald in places. Is it due to the chemo or did he do a bad job at shaving her, or getting someone to do it?

How could he do that? Being away from home and her medical treatments could be dangerous. There's only one explanation.

He wants her to die out here, with me.

"I'll do anything." I bring my hands together. "Just let her go."

"The only thing I want you to do is act like a proper wife. She's not going anywhere. If I were you, I'd stop begging. It makes you look pathetic."

"You're an asshole," I scream out, blinded by rage.

This time he doesn't respond in words. His hand meets my cheek so hard my head threatens to explode. "Don't make me remind you of what I'm capable of." He grinds the words out between his teeth. "I have only a few rules and you will follow them, both of you.".

6

He pushes his hands into his pockets and lets out a harsh breath. "The rules are simple, but once they're broken, the consequences are unbearable. I'll say this once and I never want to repeat myself again." He points at Christa. "That woman over there, is no longer your sister. She's here to work, and that's it. She's nothing but a maid. You will not, under any circumstances, offer to help her do her job, nor will you be allowed to speak to her."

"I can do the work myself." I know I'm

walking on dangerous ground, but how can I sit back and do nothing, say nothing?

"Don't test my patience, Emma." He folds his arms in front of his chest. "I know you can do the damn job, but I don't want you to. You are my wife. And frankly, I'm surprised at your reaction. Would you have preferred to have a stranger helping you?"

Yes, I want to say, but I don't dare. It would have been much easier for me to watch a stranger suffer instead of my own sister—my sick sister.

Questions race through my mind, driving me mad.

Who did he even send to kidnap her? Was it his pilot? Where was Christa when it happened? At home? At work? Was she snatched from the street?

"Let me repeat myself, one last time." He leans against the kitchen table. "From this day on, you're no longer related to that woman, and her mouth will remain sealed shut so she never speaks to you."

He kneels down next to me and grips my chin so I look into his eyes. "I'm doing this for you. I'm trying to be an amazing husband."

An amazing husband? What kind of world is he living in?

I turn my head so that my chin is no longer in the palm of his hand.

He lets out a bitter chuckle and gets up. "You don't get it, do you? This is a gift from me to you on this special day."

I glare at him, waiting for him to enlighten me.

"It's your birthday, silly. The maid is your birthday present."

I continue to stare at him, unblinking. Given what's going on around me, who cares about my birthday? I'll probably never celebrate it again after all this is over. If I make it through this ordeal alive, every time my birthday comes around, I'll always remember this place, this moment. I wish he never told me what day it is.

Christa cries softly, her shoulders shaking. I can't bear it. I can't stay away when she's hurting so bad. I ignore the consequences as I crawl to her side, press my body close to hers. Her tears drip onto my skin. I wish it were possible for me to share some of her pain.

With handcuffed hands, it's hard to hold her, but I do my best before our contact is broken. "I love you," I say even if Dax is watching.

I'm not surprised when he pulls me away. "Stop fucking with me." He knocks me to the floor again where I curl up into a ball, weeping.

Next, he goes to Christa, and wraps a hand around her neck. "Misbehave again and I'll kill her."

The sound of Christa's whimpers break my heart. But how can I help her when saving her means hurting her? I can't let her die.

This would never have happened if I died out at sea. She would have been safe. Or would she? Dax is unpredictable. He could have gone to Mistport to harm her anyway, just because he can.

I blink away the tears and struggle to pull myself to my feet and onto a chair. "Okay," I say to Dax, my voice in pieces. "I'll follow your rules if you promise not to hurt her."

"That's what I like to hear." He drops into a chair and pulls a cigarette from his pocket. I'm surprised when he lights it up and starts to smoke. I had no idea he's smoking again.

Watching him reminds me of when I saw him on the Mistport movie set. I remember the smoke curling up into the sky. Even though I knew smoking is a nasty habit, it had looked sexy on him. I was completely turned on. I should have known what he was then. Something or someone out there should have warned me.

"I have a little secret." He blows a cloud of smoke in my direction. "You'd be glad to hear that your maid doesn't have cancer, not anymore. She was misdiagnosed this time." He shrugs. "I might as well tell you since she can't do it herself."

At hearing those words, I'm overwhelmed with so much joy and fear at the same time that I cannot stop myself from touching my sister again, showing her how grateful I am that she will live. In the darkness that surrounds me, that piece of good news is the light at the end of the tunnel. As Christa tries to hold onto my hand, Dax shoots from his chair so fast I don't see him coming.

I cry out when he grabs me. The next sensation is a sharp pain at the back of my neck. The smell of burning flesh and hair fills the air.

My hand goes to the back of my head, but I can't touch the spot because my skin is still screaming with pain.

"I warned you." He tosses the cigarette to the floor and crushes it with his foot. "Don't test me again."

Christa is screaming as well behind the tape, her body writhing in the chair, her head lolling from side to side. She hears my pain and I know she wants to help me. But she's completely helpless.

I can't stop Dax as he charges toward her and slaps her hard across the face. That shuts her up immediately. Her pain reaches me and sinks into my heart. I know how his palm feels against the skin. My sobs grow louder as I watch Christa's cheek redden in response to the assault.

How did we end up here? We had dreams and hopes for the future. They didn't involve us being trapped on a farm by a psychopath.

Dax keeps us in the kitchen for hours without food or drink. Like Christa, I'm also handcuffed to the chair now. He has positioned us in such a way that we're sitting opposite each other, looking into each other's eyes, unable to communicate in words or to touch.

When the sun finally sets, Dax prepares himself a salad and enjoys it in front of us.

He wants to teach us a lesson, to remind us—especially me—who's in charge. He wants us to know we have no chance against him.

But he should know by now that I'm a fighter. Yesterday, I may have been weak, but today things are different. He does not know that bringing my sister here is actually a blessing in disguise. Christa has given me a reason to fight. As I watch the pain reflected on her face, I find my will to live.

If she hadn't shown up, maybe I would have given up eventually. But she needs to live. Without the cancer holding her back, she deserves a chance to start over, to live a good life. Dax has made a huge mistake and he doesn't even know it yet.

When night falls, he takes Christa out of the chair. "I'll lock her in her room," he says and walks out with her swaying by his side. "It's right next to our own bedroom."

A few minutes later, he comes back for me.

The first thing he does once he handcuffs me to the bed is go to the wall. He presses his ear against it. "She must be so upset," he says to me with a grin. "I can hear her crying. Don't worry, she'll get used to it."

Back on the bed, he kisses me. His tongue parts my lips and thrusts into my mouth. I tense up when his hands sweep across my body and stop at the elastic of my panties.

Afraid he might hurt Christa if I reject him, I lie still. He stops kissing me and places himself between my legs. He pulls down my panties and groans. Then he climbs off me and goes to his side of the bed. He must have seen a bit of blood there. I'm sure it's not much, but it's enough to turn him off.

It's such a relief to me. It would have killed me to have him inside me.

He's lying on his back now, his hands behind his head. His jaw is tight, too pissed off to even speak.

I pull my panties back up with my free hand and turn away from him. I think of Christa in the other room, broken and in pain.

My mind keeps going back to the expression on her face when I saw her in the kitchen today. I remember the tears, her sealed lips, the questions in her eyes. She has been through enough pain.

I have to rescue her from Dax. If he kills me for saving her, it would all be worth it. My death would be a small price to pay for saving the one person who means the world to me.

If I'm lucky, one day she will find a way to forgive me for all the mistakes I made, mistakes that brought this on to her. I will certainly never be able to forgive myself. No matter what I do for her, it will never be enough to erase the pain I have caused.

7

Unlike Dax who's snoring next to me, I cannot find the peace to fall asleep, not after what happened today. With each breath I take, my need to escape grows stronger. I want to grab Christa and run. But where do I even start?

I turn to look at my captor. It's too dark for me to see his features, but the shape of his face is enough to make my blood boil. How does he do it? How is he able to sleep knowing he has destroyed or taken so many lives?

While I watch him, something catches my eye, a flashing light on his nightstand.

The soft green glow spreads through the darkness like a light at the end of the tunnel. It has to be coming from his phone.

Before bed, I saw him remove it from his pocket to place it on the nightstand. My fingers itch to snatch it and call for help. But the distance is too great between me and the only thing that might be able to help.

The phone is so near, yet so far out of reach. He put it there knowing full well it will torture me to see it and not be able to get to it.

A noise cuts through my thoughts. It's coming from the other side of the wall. Christa is awake and her strangled sobs are clearly audible. Her cries break through the wall and hit my core.

I suppress a whimper that makes its way up my hitching chest. If only I had the strength to break the chains Dax had put around us. If only I could do something. But what?

I move my hand to one of my ears. I can't bear the sound of her pain. I wish I could shut it off. I know she's weeping for both of us.

When we were kids she was my protector. If anyone had dared to hurt me, they got a piece of her. Now she's as helpless as I am, and I caused her this pain. The broken look in her eyes had killed me. The once strong and confident woman was nowhere to be seen in the depth of her eyes.

It will be all right, Christa. I'll figure something out. I promise.

The light from Dax's phone dies, only to awaken again seconds later. Someone must be desperate to reach him.

As hard as it is to see his phone and not be able to get to it, it's comforting to know he brought one with him. It's only a matter of time before I get close enough to take it and call for help. One day he will make a mistake and I'll be ready.

I stare at it for a long time, wondering if he's using the same number he had in LA. I doubt it. He had done too much damage to allow easy access to himself. He wouldn't want the cops to track him down. By now, the news about my kidnapping must have spread like wildfire throughout the country, if not worldwide. He would be stupid to keep the same number.

I *will* get my hands on that phone. It

might take a while, but I'll find a way to get us out of this hell.

I close my eyes and pray. I pray for me. I pray for Christa. I pray for an escape. I pray for strength to survive each day of torture. I pray for peace. I pray for Dax's downfall.

As soon as I open my eyes again, a wave of peace and calm sweeps through my entire body. It makes me feel lighter, less afraid of the dark. The pain of the burn behind my neck throbs a little less.

Christa has stopped crying now and fragile silence has fallen over the room.

The phone has stopped flashing. Now pure darkness surrounds me. I close my eyes again, force myself to fall asleep. I do eventually, but then the nightmares return. I dream of my baby.

I'm on a hospital bed, in labor with Dax by my side, our fingers intertwined. He resembles the man I used to know, the man I used to love. My feelings for him are intense as I push our baby out into the world.

Tears of joy and relief fill my eyes when the baby finally arrives with a piercing cry, and the doctor hands him or her to Dax. He's in awe as he gazes down at the tiny face. When he looks back at me, his expression has changed. The smile is gone, and his eyes are deep pools of darkness.

My heart clenches when he pulls the baby closer and turns around to walk out of the room. The doctor and nurses don't stop him, and my physical pain keeps me chained to the bed.

The door closes softly behind him, shutting me out of my baby's life.

Soon after, I emerge from the dream with tears in my eyes, the pain of loss still buried deep inside my chest. I'm crying so loud that I wake Dax.

He lets out a groan, switches on his lamp, and turns to face me. "Bad dream?" he asks.

I lick my lips and nod. When I sleep, I'm in hell. When I'm awake, I'm still in hell. There's no way out.

"I'm sorry, baby." He wraps an arm around my middle and presses his face into my neck. "You don't have to be afraid. I'm here."

I try to pull away, but he holds on

tighter. "Don't do that." His voice is firm. "You're not going anywhere. You belong in my arms." He pushes a hand to the back of my neck and I wince, feeling the burn of the cigarette hours ago.

I shove him harder away from me.

"Hey, what's the matter?" A frown appears between his eyes.

"It hurts," I say between clenched teeth. I don't need to explain to him what hurts because he already knows.

He gets out of bed and stands before me in his boxer shorts. "I'll be right back."

He leaves the room and returns moments later with a cooling pad. Even though I struggle to get away from him, he pulls me to him and presses it behind my neck. The relief it offers is only skin deep. My pain goes way past the flesh. It enters my bones and cuts into my heart. It flows like hot lava through my veins. It poisons every part of me.

"Better?" he asks.

I chew the corner of my lip. If I say yes, I'd be lying because the pain is still there, etched into my skin. If I say no, he would accuse me of being an ungrateful bitch.

Also, if I say I'm fine, I'd be giving him permission to hold me longer, and make him feel like the hero he's not.

I choose silence, my skin still hurting. As soon as he removes the cooling pad, the burning sensation returns worse than ever.

"If you were obedient, you would not be hurting right now."

"I know," I say softly. "You didn't mean to hurt me." His words, not mine. I'm only telling him what he wants to hear.

"That's right. I never mean to hurt you. You make me do it. Hurting you hurts me as well."

I purse my lips and nod. "I'm sorry, Dax."

"You should be. I'm your husband. I want to make you happy, but you're making it difficult for me. I thought you would be happy with my surprise today."

"I wasn't expecting it to be—" I press my lips together to hold back the tears. "I wasn't expecting it."

"I know." He pulls me close again and this time I don't reject him. I know his limits.

As a reward he presses his lips on my

damp cheek. "I love you."

"If you love me, don't hurt Christa. She did nothing wrong." My words are drenched in tears. "Don't kill her."

He withdraws his arms from my body and tenses next to me. "If she dies, you're at fault. It won't be on me. Whether I pull the trigger or not, the blood will be on your hands. The only way you can protect her is by being obedient. Step out of line and she could end up dead. I need you to promise that you will obey me from now on."

"I don't know what you want from me." I clench and unclench my fists. "You've taken away everything that means anything to me. You have destroyed my life, left me with nothing. My sister, she's all I have. I thought I lost her before when you told me she was dead." My skin prickles with disgust at what he put me through.

"Aren't you happy she's not? She's here. I brought her to you. Even though you're no longer allowed to call her your sister, you get to see her every day. Is it so hard to say thanks?"

"How long will she be staying with us?"

I hold my breath.

"No idea." He switches off the light. "My love, when the time comes, you'll be the first to know. When we no longer need her, it will be up to you to decide her fate."

8

When I wake up, he's already awake and getting dressed.

"Hey, baby." He stretches his arms above his head, yawning. "Did you sleep well?"

I don't give him the answer to his question. When he fell asleep last night, I was still awake for a while, thinking. I'll try harder from now on to do what he wants. Having Christa's life in my hands is terrifying as hell.

The worst thing that could happen right now is for him to throw me into the dungeon. I don't even want to imagine what he would do to Christa when I'm not around. He might take out his frustrations on her.

I have no choice but to play the game of pretend.

He bends down to kiss me on the lips, but I suddenly turn away and sneeze so he meets my cheek instead. It was not my intention, but how would he know?

I hold my breath as he watches me for a moment. My posture slumps with relief when his lips spread into a smile. "I'm in a good mood today. Seeing your face every morning does that to me." He straightens back up. "Let's have a good day today. Let's not fight again, okay?" He comes to my side of the bed and sits down. I can't wait for him to remove the handcuffs. My wrist needs a break. But he doesn't. He only checks to see if they're still closed.

He leans in to kiss me again. This time he gets my lips. Satisfied with himself, he rises to his feet and goes to the bathroom. I listen to him brushing his teeth, wishing I could do the same to remove the sour taste from my mouth.

After a while, he exits the bathroom. In his hand is a toothbrush with toothpaste smeared on top of it. He sits back down next to me and raises it to my lips. I try to take it from him, to brush my own teeth.

He shakes his head. "Allow me." His breath smells minty.

Aware that this could be another one of his tests, I show him my teeth and allow him to do the job. His brushing is rough and sometimes he pushes the toothbrush so deep into my mouth that I gag. He doesn't even seem to notice my discomfort.

To intensify the brushing, he slides his hand to the back of my neck, the place he burned, and draws me nearer.

I want to grit my teeth to better deal with the pain, but then I would be biting on the toothbrush.

"Done," he says finally and uses a facecloth to wipe the foam from around my lips.

He returns the toothbrush and facecloth to the bathroom. I listen to him moving things around in there while I wait with bated breath for him to return, to take me to Christa.

He emerges from the bathroom and orders me to go and urinate, which is a relief until he insists on wiping me himself. I hate what he's doing to me. He's so skilled at making me feel even more vulnerable to him.

Once he's done, he handcuffs me the way he had done yesterday, my hands in front of me. Then he pulls me to my feet. I can barely stand given that I hardly slept last night. But I have to push through the pain and discomfort to get to Christa.

He takes me to the kitchen and lowers me into the same chair I had occupied yesterday.

"I'll get the maid," he says and disappears from the kitchen again. The sound of that word makes me sick to my stomach.

An invisible dagger plunges into my heart at the sound of my sister crying. I hear her pain before I get to see her again.

She looks even more broken than yesterday, her face crumpled, her eyes swollen and red, her skin pale. She reminds me of the time she was going through the chemo treatments. Those treatments had always weakened her so much that she became a shell of herself.

He helps her into one of the chairs and turns the chair to face me. "Emma, tell her what you want for breakfast."

Christa watches me with empty eyes, waiting for me to respond. I can't. As much as I want to obey Dax, I cannot bring myself to treat my sister like a maid.

"I'm not hungry," I mumble under my breath.

"Come on, babe. You must be starving. You didn't get much to eat yesterday. How about something light? You'll not be inconveniencing anyone. I'm sure it won't be hard for the maid to figure out how to cook over an open fire."

Christa's eyes meet mine, questioning. I know what she's thinking.

Ignoring us, Dax goes to the fridge. He removes eggs and several other ingredients that could be used to make breakfast. He dumps everything on the table in front of Christa.

"Well, if you're not hungry, I am. Get up and make breakfast, slave," he barks.

It takes all my strength not to jump to my feet and attack him for calling my sister a slave. But am I ready for the consequences?

I suppress a shudder as he leads us to the kitchen area he had set up outside.

He positions Christa in front of the three stones, which now frame a small mountain of ashes.

From where I'm sitting, I'm humiliated at the sight of my sister's bare behind. I don't even want to imagine how she feels. Dax uses nakedness to make us weak and vulnerable.

Dax pulls a box of matches from his pocket and hands them to Christa. When he brings a pan from the kitchen and balances it on top of the stones, Christa stares at the fireplace in disbelief. She's a chef by profession, and I know she will be able to pull it off, but I'm certain she didn't expect to be cooking over an open fire. I hope she will remember her skills from when we went camping during school.

"What are you waiting for?" Dax barks.

Christa glances at me briefly, then drops to her knees in front of the stones.

It takes her a while to make the fire, and Dax offers her no help. He doesn't even remove the handcuffs to make the job easier.

I want to jump from my chair, to turn on Dax. But I remind myself of what he said last night. If she dies, it will be my fault.

As though she can feel my pain, Christa looks at me again and gives me the tiniest of nods. Without words, she's sending a message to me, assuring me she's fine. I sigh with relief when I finally see a glow between the rocks with a small flame dancing from it. The smoke rises into her eyes and she blinks away the burn.

"What's taking you so long?" Dax jams a hand into his hair.

"It's hard for her," I whisper, but he's close enough to hear the words.

"That's it. I've had it with you." He lunges at me and pulls me to my feet by the neck. "Looks like it's time for you to get a taste of the dungeon."

He uses his free hand to grab Christa by the apron. The next moment, we're both stumbling forward into the kitchen, bumping against furniture. I hate that it's not the final destination. I don't even have a chance to warn Christa about the dungeon.

In the hallway, Dax plants his hands between our shoulder blades and pushes us forward. Sometimes we bump against walls, other times into each other. Neither of us makes a sound, fearing he would punish us more.

The closer we come to the dungeon, the harder it becomes for me to breathe. Anxiety gnaws at my insides when I think of Christa entering the dungeon. She's even more terrified of snakes than I am.

When we get to the door of the dungeon, Dax shoves us forward so hard we drop to our knees. He leaves us on the floor until he has unlocked the door, then one after the other, he pulls us to our feet and throws us into the prison.

I choke back a scream. Christa still doesn't make a sound, but I know she will once the lights go on. If only I could keep her in the dark.

I'm already shifting from foot to foot, aware of the danger underneath my feet.

I'm not sure if it's only in my head, but I think I hear the sound of snakes hissing. The thought that there might be some holes in the glass causes me to pant in terror.

"Each time one of you misbehaves, you will both be punished," his voice booms from the other side of the door. At the same time, the light goes on and Christa finally sees the snakes. She jumps to her feet so fast that she falls back down, only to scramble back up again to get away from the snakes. But there's no escape.

Something about the sight of snakes makes me want to throw up again, my stomach clenching and unclenching. I refuse to give in to the urge. Christa cannot see my weakness. I have to be strong for both of us.

We both huddle by the door, the sound of Christa's sobs shredding my heart. She grabs the door handle and tries to lift herself off the floor with its help, but the handle is too small and she's much too weak to hold on for long.

We both turn to the sound of something sliding open. For the first time I notice a small glass window not too far from the door. Dax's face appears, his features shrouded in smoke. "How do you like that?" He lowers the cigarette from his lips.

While Christa presses herself against the door, I close my eyes, reminding myself that the danger is on the other side of the glass. As long as the glass is intact, the snakes cannot hurt us.

When I open my eyes again, Dax is gone and Christa is leaning into me for the protection I don't have the power to give.

"Don't look down," I say quickly, but her eyes are still glued to the floor.

Sweat breaks through her pale skin as she pushes herself against the wall. The look on her face will haunt me forever. I've never seen her so afraid; she looks about to pass out. Guilt stabs me in the chest.

What have I done to her? What if she doesn't survive this ordeal?

9

Long after Dax throws us into the dungeon, Christa's fear still consumes both of us. Exhausted from jumping up and down, she's now huddled in a crumpled heap next to me. Even though she has figured out that it's less terrifying to look up instead of down, her body still twitches and shifts from time to time, desperate for escape.

Despite being only a few inches away from each other, we're not touching.

Dax is back at the window, watching us. He doesn't look like he's planning to leave anytime soon.

I ache to break the handcuffs and pull my sister into my arms, to hold her tight, to assure her that she doesn't have to be afraid, that I will protect her. But I can't do that with him watching us like a hawk.

I'm desperate to talk to Christa, to hear her voice. I have no idea what I would say to her, and I'm nervous to hear what she has to say. I fear she might point out the obvious, that it's all my fault. At the same time, I want her to say something so she can feel like a normal person again.

Sooner or later Dax will disappear from the window to get something to eat or use the bathroom. Or he would simply get bored with watching us. When he does, I will grab the chance to connect with Christa.

At the thought of Dax going to the bathroom, my bladder starts to complain. The urge to urinate is so intense tears spring to my eyes. As his prisoner, I'm only allowed to use the toilet twice a day, once in the morning and before bed.

When the stench of urine reaches my nostrils, I think it's mine. But it's not. I'm still hanging in there. The smell must be coming from Christa. My heart goes out to her. I've been there, I have been so terrified that I wet myself. I'd felt the same humiliation she probably feels now.

Dax finally disappears from the window and I let out a breath of relief.

My hands are clasped in my lap as I listen to his footsteps fading down the hall. I have no idea whether there are cameras in here, if he will see what I'm about to do, but I can't stop myself.

I scoot closer to Christa until our bodies touch, pressed into each other in some form of awkward hug.

"We'll survive this, sis. I won't let him kill us. I'll get us out of here." I pray that I'll be able to keep my promise to her, that we won't leave this farm in body bags.

I press my forehead against her damp cheek, her tears gluing us together.

Without thinking, I reach up and tug at the corner of the tape on her mouth. It takes a few tries before it lets go of her skin. I don't remove it completely, only enough for her to be able to get some words out. I have no idea how long she has been silenced for and I want to give her a chance to feel a bit human again before Dax returns.

"Oh, my God," she says, her voice

breaking. "Oh, my God."

"I know, Christa. I know. But we can't panic right now. We have to stay strong."

"I'm scared." Her voice is so small she sounds like a frightened child. "I don't want to die, Emma. I don't—"

"You won't. I won't let that happen." My hands clutch her arm. "I'll get you out of here."

As soon as I hear the footsteps again, a sign that Dax is coming back, I quickly put the tape back in place. She doesn't struggle, but her body tenses up and she's blinking furiously.

I move away from her before Dax arrives, then I bring my hands to my lap again and stare straight ahead at the empty wall in front of me, trying to ignore the deadly snakes lurking beneath us. It's hard to ignore the deadliest of them all, the one on the other side of the door.

When I feel his presence back at the small window, I don't want to, but I find myself turning to look. My furious eyes meet his head on and he smiles. Then, he steps away. As soon as his face disappears out of sight, the light goes out. Christa starts to struggle again.

The fear I had been stifling suddenly explodes in my body, but I do my best to pull myself together. If Christa senses my fear, hers will shoot to another level.

It's a struggle to keep it together when there are dangerous creatures beneath my feet, some of them brushing against the glass. What if the glass is not strong enough to carry our weight and it somehow cracks?

I glance at the window where Dax had been standing. No one is there.

I can't help thinking that he knows I spoke to Christa. Maybe he even heard every word I said to her. Maybe leaving us in the dark is the punishment. I have a feeling he will stay away for a while.

I bite hard into my bottom lip and slide myself against the wall on my way to Christa. I should probably stay where I am, but my body refuses to listen to my head. I need to be near her, to comfort her the best I can.

When I get to her, I lean into her body. "I'm so sorry," I utter through my tears. "I'm really sorry, Christa."

In response to my words, she presses her cheek to mine. Her body has stopped trembling now, as though the darkness has calmed her down a bit. Maybe it helps that she no longer has to see the snakes. It must be easier for her to imagine they're not there. It is for me.

"He won't kill us," I repeat, hoping she will believe me. "We'll get back home, okay?"

I want to hear her response, to know whether she trusts me, but it's too risky for me to remove the tape again, even though that would only be one rule of the many I have already broken.

Christa responds by resting her head on my shoulder. That's enough for now.

After a few minutes, I move away in case Dax switches the light back on.

Nothing happens for a long time and then suddenly, I detect a change in the air. It's cooler, much cooler. It reminds me of the time on the yacht when Dax sucked warmth out of my room to punish me. Is he doing the same thing now? He must be because the temperature seems to be dropping at a fast rate. From Christa's increased whimpers, I know she feels it too.

Now that circumstances have changed, I return to her and we huddle up together again, this time in search of warmth.

On the other side of the wall, we hear laughter. He must be watching, as I suspected he would. It's a small relief that he's not returning to pull us apart.

"I love you, Christa," I whisper into the darkness. "Whatever happens, remember that I love you. I hope one day you'll forgive me."

Christa is trembling now, and no matter how close we get to each other, how much I wish I could keep her warm, it doesn't work. She's making desperate, inaudible sounds behind the tape as if she's trying to tell me something. Maybe she wants me to know that she loves me too, that she forgives me.

I close my eyes tight, only to open them again when his laughter grows louder. He's coming back.

I pull away from Christa immediately but it's too late. The light is back on and his face is at the window.

"Since you still haven't learned your lesson, you'll be spending the rest of the day and night in there." Still laughing, he allows darkness to fall again. The sound of his footsteps follows him down the hallway.

A few minutes later, the same music he had tortured me with on the yacht, pours into the room, louder than I've ever heard it before, so loud that my head aches from listening to it.

Christa is screaming behind the tape. I don't need to hear her to know that. Her pain pierces through me like a sword.

I press my hands between my legs, trying to get my thighs to warm me up. Dax is just getting started. I know that better than anyone else. Am I really strong enough to handle whatever will come next or am I kidding myself?

This time it's Christa who comes to me, her cool hands touching my arm. She clutches onto my hands, reminding me of how things used to be when we were kids. When mom and dad fought, she always came to my room to comfort me, like she's doing now. I'm her little sister again, terrified of the monsters in the dark. Only this time, the monsters are also in the light. They are real.

As time passes, and we continue to hold on to each other, sleep starts to pull me under. It's a good thing. If I fall asleep, maybe time would speed up. On the other hand, I'm also terrified of being unconscious with deadly creatures near me. What if Dax breaks the glass while I'm sleeping and I wake up to the bite of a snake?

But when sleep is determined to knock you out, it's hard to fight it. Finally, my eyes close without me even knowing it.

When I open them again, I have no idea how much time has passed, but the air is a touch warmer and instead of complete darkness, the light is being switched on and off over and over again. One look at Christa tells me something has changed in her.

Her body is present, but she's staring into space, no longer reacting to what's going on around her. I nudge her a little, but she still doesn't move. The good news is, she's still breathing. Maybe it's best to allow her to handle the shock in her own way, by checking out for a while.

Right now, I wish I could do the same. But it wouldn't be a good idea for both of us to escape into our minds. I have to stay on guard. Since I'm the one who started all this in the first place, I should be the one who stays back to fight the war.

10

When the light stops flashing and the music dies, I'm just as numb as Christa, staring into space like a zombie, my head clouded from lack of sleep.

I spent hours—at least that's what it feels like—whispering into Christa's ear, repeating promises I'm not sure I'll be able to keep.

I'm almost relieved when the familiar thud of his footfalls echoes from down the hall.

Christa, who is suddenly alert, moves away from me only seconds before Dax appears behind the small window. Instead of looking up at him, her gaze drops to the floor. Even though she sees the snakes, this time she doesn't react. Has her fear numbed her?

Through the window, Dax seems pleased with himself. He must have just stepped out of the shower because his hair looks damp and darker than usual, his face covered in a smile as he chews on something. Watching him, my stomach rumbles with hunger.

He thinks he has finally broken us. Maybe he has, for now.

I wouldn't have minded so much if it were only me suffering at his hands. His torture is not new to me. I'm used to all the humiliation. But it's different for Christa. It's her first contact with the devil.

He nears the glass, presses his forehead against the pane. "Ready to follow the rules now?"

Christa glances first at me, then at Dax. She gives a small nod. I follow her lead. It feels like the right thing to do for now.

My body folds with relief when the door opens. I don't even make a sound when Dax pulls me to my feet.

As he had done yesterday, he pushes us down the hallway, our weak bodies crashing against the walls, our knees hitting the floor before he picks us up again.

He first allows us to use the toilet, and then throws us out into the morning sunshine. It's so bright that my eyes hurt. The sky above is blue and untainted. The world looks innocent, and quiet, and safe. Yet, there's an evil lurking below the surface.

In front of us is a massive, silver tub filled with water. A pile of dirty laundry lies next to it. At close inspection I notice clothes, bed sheets, and the filthy curtains I'd seen around the house.

"Get to work, slave." Dax waves a hand at the pile. "Those things won't wash themselves." He pins Christa with a look of disdain. "What are you waiting for?"

He doesn't offer to remove the handcuffs so that she can do the job comfortably. His intention is to make her suffer. I know for sure he doesn't even need any of the things that had belonged to the previous owner. He's simply exercising his power, torturing me by torturing her.

Resigned to her fate, Christa steps forward and reaches down with both hands to lift one of the dirty sheets. Then she drops to her knees in front of the tub, gazing into the water for a few seconds.

I know what she's thinking. Like me, she's so thirsty she wishes she could drink it. Her hand is shaking when she picks up the bottle of laundry detergent. It's hard for her to open it with handcuffs on, but she does her best, then pours some of the blue liquid into the tub. She uses both hands to spread the soap in the water.

Finally, she reaches for a filthy curtain and dips it into the water. She faces us so her behind is not on display.

Guilt consumes me from within. I want to offer to switch places with her, but the price of disobedience is one we would both end up paying.

So I stand next to Dax, helpless as I watch her wash. I try to look away, but Dax turns my head to look at my sister's struggle.

When it gets too hard for her to wash with her hands, she climbs into the tub and tramples the fabrics clean. Our maternal grandmother used to wash her bedspreads and comforters that way. When we visited her, she would fill the bath with water and let us have a go as well.

Once Christa trampled the dirt from the fabrics, she gets out of the tub, her face shiny with sweat. She uses her hands again to remove stubborn marks, then struggles to wring the water out. What feels like hours later, the washing is done and hung on the clothesline outside the kitchen.

Christa is still determined to obey as Dax orders her to cook lunch. This time, it doesn't take her long to light the fire. Her eyes are dry, even though my own tears trickle down my cheeks.

She prepares a meal of roasted meat, rice, and steamed vegetables, a meal Dax doesn't even offer her.

Unable to bear the look of hunger in her eyes as she watches us eat, I know I need to do or say something.

I inhale a dose of courage and steel myself for whatever will happen once I speak up. "Dax... sweetheart, give her something to eat, please. She needs her strength, so she can work."

Dax continues to eat in silence. Then he nods. "You have a point. I'll get her some bread." He goes back into the kitchen and returns with three slices of white bread.

When he yanks the tape from Christa's mouth and gives her the food, she shoves it into her mouth and barely chews it before swallowing it down.

"How about a drink?" I ask, hoping he won't get pissed off.

He throws me a look, but grabs the bottle of water at his feet and hands it to me. "Don't give her too much."

My heart splinters as I hold the bottle while Christa drinks from it greedily, her hands tight around it. Some of the water pours to the ground because she's drinking too fast.

"Enough," Dax orders, but I don't stop. I tip the bottle so more water can get into her mouth.

"I said enough." The thread of warning in his voice causes me to turn around, to see the handgun he's pointing at me. "Do as I say, or you will both be dead."

"Okay, okay." I remove Christa's hands from around the bottle and stand, my stomach churning with fear. "I've stopped, okay?"

"Good." Dax lowers the gun to his lap. "But since she had more than enough to drink, she won't get any more water until tomorrow."

That won't happen. I will not let him do that.

Christa doesn't say a word as she shoves another piece of bread into her mouth, moments before Dax grabs the rest and tosses it onto his own plate. He grabs her head again and tapes her mouth shut while she's still chewing, and I force down a sick feeling.

After lunch, Christa washes the dishes while I'm handcuffed to a chair at the kitchen table, forced to watch her while Dax smokes in the doorway.

Christa gets the job done without even a glance at me. She's acting strong, but I sense her pain and see the teardrops dripping into the sink.

When she's done with the washing up, Dax grabs her by the neck and takes her back to her room. The sounds of the door slamming against the wall, the clink of her handcuffs, and her groans of pain, cause my lungs to constrict, making it hard to breathe. The door is slammed shut again, then there's silence.

A terrible thought sneaks into my mind. Please God, don't let him do anything to her. What if he rapes her?

"Dax," I call out, trying to release myself from the chair. "Dax, come back. Don't. . . please don't touch her."

My stomach is in knots in the time it takes for him to return to the kitchen.

He's zipping up his pants when he reenters the room.

Bitterness fills my stomach. "No," I shake my head. "You didn't—"

"I didn't what? Fuck her?" He dips his head to one side. "Why not?"

"You wouldn't." Tears plop onto my lap. "You wouldn't." I'm so broken I can barely form a full sentence.

He comes to put a hand on my head. "Calm down." He throws his head back and roars with laughter. "I didn't fuck the bitch. I was in the bathroom after I dropped her off. That's what took me so long." He runs his hand in circles over my scalp. "The truth is, I was playing a game. I actually wanted you to think I had sex with her."

Fucking bastard. I'm both relieved and furious at him for putting me through those few minutes of hell. Thank God he didn't rape her. I don't know what I would have done if he had.

"I love to see you jealous." He kisses the top of my head. "It shows that you love me."

I don't say anything to burst his bubble. Let him believe what he wants to. It doesn't change how I feel about him, how much I despise him.

I'm at least glad that even though Christa is locked up, she will at least have a break from him. I hope she'll be able to get some rest.

The rest of the day, Christa remains in her prison of a room and Dax pretends to be a caring husband, showing me around the farm, introducing me to the horses at the stables.

"I'll teach you to ride one day. It's so liberating."

His words come from a distance away. My mind is not with him at all, but with Christa, though I do my best to respond at the right times so I don't get punished again.

By the end of the day, I'm exhausted with worry about how Christa is doing inside the room. I hate that I cannot check up on her. She must be so hungry and thirsty.

So we both don't get punished, I tuck my pain away and wait for whatever comes next. When the sun starts to go down, I pray he'll bring her out to come and prepare dinner. That way I'll be able to see if she's okay. But Dax cooks dinner himself.

He lays it out on the kitchen table and places a candle in the middle. His attempt at romance falls flat.

When Dax sees I'm barely touching my food, feeling guilty to be eating while Christa starves, he comes to feed me himself, shoving the boiled potatoes down my throat. Everything tastes like cardboard to me.

Later in bed, he wraps his arms around me. From the other side of the wall I can hear Christa weeping. On one hand it's good to know she's still alive, but on the other, her sorrow shreds my insides.

Instead of crying or falling asleep, I think of a plan of action that would get us away from Dax forever. My impulsive ways are what have brought us to this place. I have to stop just reacting to things. If I want to survive, I need to be a different person, to do things I have never done before. I have no choice but to become the person I used to think was boring, someone who is responsible. I have to think like Christa.

For the first time in my life I understand the value of thinking things through before I act, the value of planning. Dax always has a plan. He's always one step ahead. I need to find a way to beat him at his game of cat and mouse.

.

11
―――

I wake up before the sun comes out, still determined to find a way out of Dax's life. The discomfort of the handcuffs around my wrist and the burn of the cigarette at the back of my neck, pushes me to focus on escaping. But most of all I have to do if for Christa.

As terrifying as it is to stand up to Dax, the alternative is scarier. The only other way out is death. I'm not about to go down without a fight.

Dax is still asleep next to me, an arm flung above his head while one of mine is handcuffed to the bed. The sound of his breathing makes my stomach turn with disgust. I have never shot a gun, but if I had access to one right now, I would pull the trigger without a second thought.

I lay on my back, searching my clouded mind for some kind of idea.

By the time he stirs, I still don't know what I'm going to do. He turns to face me, puts an arm around my body. When he kisses my neck, a shiver runs through me. I cannot bear to have him near me.

My desperation to get away intensifies the urge to escape. An idea finally drops into my mind. I know what I have to do.

"Dax?"

"Yeah?" His voice is muffled as his mouth is still pressed against my skin.

"I need to ask you a favor." Before I can lose the courage, I get to the point. "I'm begging you to let Christa go. I'll do anything in return." I stress the word "anything".

He stops kissing me and looks into my face. "What do you mean by anything?"

"Anything. . . Anything you want." My hands tighten into fists. "If you give me the chance, I'll be the best wife to you. If you want sex every day, you've got it." He doesn't know yet that the bleeding has completely stopped. Yesterday, when I found the pad I was wearing clean, I grieved silently for my unborn child. Now that the blood is gone, the baby is only a memory.

Dax pushes himself up on an elbow. "I love the sound of that." His hand moves across the sheets to my breast. He squeezes a little too tight, but I don't move a muscle. "Show me first how grateful you'll be if I let her go."

I squeeze my eyes tight. Can I really do this? Do I have a choice? I open my eyes again and meet his gaze. "I want to make love to you but not with handcuffs on. They hurt my wrists."

He hesitates for a moment. His hands move away from my body and he turns to gaze at the ceiling. Good. He's giving it some thought.

Without saying a word, he gets out of bed and comes to my side with the key to the handcuffs. He inserts it into the tiny lock and sets me free.

As soon as I'm no longer bound to the bed, he falls over me like an animal in heat. I don't push him away. Instead, I make myself reach for him. This is a small price to pay for freedom.

"I've missed you so damn much." His tongue licks my neck, then my face. I shut my eyes so I don't see the lust in his eyes.

I make all the right noises to pretend I'm enjoying myself, moaning as his hands sweep past parts of me that were once sensitive to his touch but are now numb from hate and pain.

I try not to be too loud. The last thing I need is for Christa to know I'm sleeping with the enemy. She might not understand.

When his mouth comes to my lips, a wave of disgust rushes through me, but instead of paying attention to it, I push my fingers into his hair to pull him closer. I kiss him like I've never kissed him or anyone before. In my mind I pretend I'm back in Hollywood, acting in a movie.

He breaks the kiss to gaze into my eyes, his skin flushed. "My wife is back. You have no idea how happy that makes me." He kisses my forehead. "Now let's make up for lost time."

He only stops to slide a condom on before covering me again with his body.

I'm not close to ready when he tears through me and I bite back a scream to contain the pain.

I don't have to wish he would speed up, because he's barely taking a breath. Inside my head I count his thrusts until it's over.

There's a sick grin on his face the entire time he slams into me. The look of victory tells me he thinks he won, that he has broken me to the point I have no choice but to give in to him completely.

His sweat coats my skin, making me want to shove him away. I find it hard to believe this is the same man whose touch used to make me go crazy with longing.

In the early stages of our relationship, he used to be so gentle, so loving. I never thought his love was the dangerous kind, a deadly obsession. But he's an actor. He gave the best performance of his life. He fooled everyone around him, including me. He walked through each day with a smirk on his face, pretending he was the man everyone thought he was. Without his mask on, he's just ugly.

As he pumps into me, his dick growing harder inside my body, I swear to myself that once I'm out of here, I'll drag his name through the mud and make sure he's locked up for the rest of his life.

I was always taught to forgive, by a mother who forgave my father for every hurtful thing he did to her. I'm not her. I cannot forgive this. If my mother were alive, she would understand.

One day, when Dax is behind bars where he belongs, I'll visit him, often. I'll look into his eyes from across the bars. I'll smile and tell him I'm glad he's no longer hurting anyone with his words and his toxic touch. I'll go back day after day to watch him rot in prison.

When Dax is close to orgasm, his fingers wrap around my wrists, awakening the pain left there by the handcuffs. I try not to scream out, but a whimper escapes. He takes that as a sign that I'm enjoying myself and picks up his pace.

His eyes are closed now and sweat is building on his forehead. I continue to watch him until he reaches the finish line. Veins pop through the skin of his neck and forehead, his eyes squeezed tight as he roars, then collapses on top of me.

It doesn't matter that I didn't come. I never want to have any more pleasure from him. No amount will ever be able to dilute the pain he has caused me.

He rolls off me and I pull in a breath, relieved it's over, for now.

He rests his chin on his hand and smiles at me. "I might have to get you on the pill. We wouldn't want to deal with another pregnancy."

I stifle my anger in case I do something that could get me into trouble.

"Will you let her go?" I ask. That's the only thing that's important to me right now.

He swipes a hand across his forehead to remove the sweat. "You really think I'm that stupid?" He shakes his head. "I love you, Emma but I don't trust you. I used to once. I believed in us. Then it all changed. You changed."

My chest tightens as my eyes plead with him. "Please, you promised."

"I didn't promise you a thing. You offered to make love to me, which is your duty as my wife. I don't have to give you anything in return."

"You keep saying you love me," I retort. "If you do, you'll do this for me." As the words pour out of my mouth, tumbling over each other, another thought comes to mind, another idea. "You brought us here because you wanted us to be alone. Let's do that. I'll make this a beautiful home for us. Whatever you want, I will do it."

"Do you mean that?" He narrows his eyes.

"More than anything." The lie comes easy, fueled by desperation and fear.

"Fine, here's what's going to happen." He blows out a breath. "Your sister can stop working for us, but she's not going anywhere. Remember the shed I showed you near the stables? It will be her new home. She will stay there until she dies. That's the best I can do."

My stomach cramps in reaction to the horror he has painted in front of my eyes. Oh, my God, what have I done? Did I make a mistake? What if I'm speeding up Christa's death instead of saving her?

"Why? Why do you need to do that? I don't. . . I don't understand."

"Because she can't leave this place. She'll

mess everything up for us." He puts his hands behind his head and sighs. "That's the only offer on the table, take it or leave it." He draws nearer to me and kisses the tip of my nose. "Now that you've made me see that it's actually better for us to be alone, I don't want anyone else around. You know what?" He inspects his fingernails. "I'll add in a little something extra. I'll lock her up with one small bottle of water, that way you can enjoy her presence on this earth for a while, even if you won't get to see her. In return, you'll be the best fucking wife, just as you promised."

12

I'm a crying mess as I beg Dax to change his mind, even telling him I'm fine with Christa continuing on as a maid. But it's too late. He has made a decision and is sticking to it.

When the sun comes out, he handcuffs me again and kisses me softly on the lips. "This is the best thing for everyone. Thank you for the great fuck."

He goes to take a shower while I sit on the bed, my head spinning out of control, tears warming my cheeks. I can't believe I've pulled the trigger that could kill my sister. What if she doesn't survive? She's already so weak. How far can one small bottle of water go? As thirsty as she must be by now, she would probably drink it in one go and have nothing left to keep her alive.

I look around me, searching for something to strike him with when he gets out of the shower. But there's nothing within my reach. Even if I hit him, how would I be able to run when I'm handcuffed to the bed?

I still haven't found a solution when he returns to the bedroom, a white towel wrapped around his waist. He looks the way he had looked when I met him for the first time at the Baroque Hotel. He had looked so handsome then. Now he's nothing but a beautiful monster.

He removes the towel from his waist and uses it to dry his hair. His head of hair reminds me of my shaved head. Done, he dresses quickly, then takes me to Christa's room. His hand is gentle on my back, but I still feel the burn of his palm.

I hope Christa will see what I was trying to do, that she will know I was only trying to protect her. I wish I could ask for her forgiveness in case it's the last time we'll see each other. But I can't do that with

Dax around.

There's a single bed in the room, but she's lying on the floor close to the door. Was she trying to escape? When she looks up, her eyes are blank and swollen, her skin ashen. Since she's unable to stand, Dax helps her to her feet.

"We have a new home for you," he says. "It was your sister's idea."

My stomach clenches as Christa glances at me, a soft frown between her eyebrows.

Please forgive me, I say inside my head, hoping the words will somehow reach her.

I wish I could do something about this, change the turn of events. But Dax has made it clear he won't change his mind. If I keep pushing, he might kill her instead.

He ushers both of us outside and into the truck. Within minutes, we're at the stables and my eyes are on the shed he was talking about. Unfortunately, it's made of brick rather than some other material—such as wood—that could be destroyed easily to create an escape.

Dax throws open the door and shoves Christa inside. There's a dirty, silver bowl on the floor. He pours the water he brought with him into it. Most of it spills onto the floor. I can barely breathe as I watch him wrestle her to the ground and unlock the handcuffs. He also removes the tape from around her mouth.

He leaves her lying there, her eyes panicked as she meets my gaze.

Dax slams the door shut and locks it from outside to break our contact. Christa's screams cut through the air and slice through my heart.

Standing heartbroken outside the door, unable to reach her, I renew my promise. I won't let her die. I will do whatever it takes.

Dax bundles me back into the truck and drives off. As the vehicle jumps over potholes, I cry uncontrollably.

"I don't get why you're upset," he says, his eyes on the path ahead. "It was your idea."

"No." Tears fly everywhere as I shake my head. "It was not my idea to lock her in the shed, to wait for her to die."

"But you wanted us to be alone. You and me with no one else interfering in our love life. From now on, that's how it will be."

I grit my teeth to stop myself from saying anything more.

Fine. I'll do whatever he wants. I'll be the best wife. But secretly, I'll be working on a plan that will blow his mind. The countdown as far as I'm concerned has just started.

It's over for Dax Pierce. Someone is going to die, and it won't be my sister. I'll kill him before she dies of dehydration. He has dug his own grave.

I'm prepared to become a monster to fight the monster.

When we get back to the house, he throws me onto the couch. I'm still unable to stop the tears. I pull up my legs and rest my chin on my knees, my tears dripping onto my flesh and trickling down my skin.

"This is ridiculous," he shouts, pacing the room. "How can you have a new family when you're still linked to the old one? We're married, for God's sake."

I still don't waste my breath reasoning with him. I have done enough damage.

In between the sobs, I imagine hearing Christa's voice from a distance. But it's impossible. She's too weak to scream so loud. The only reason I'm hearing her is because we're connected. Her pain is my pain. Her tears are my tears.

It will not be long until it's over, until I get her out of there. I have to find the best way to finish Dax off. I can't wait to look him straight in the eye when he perishes.

By locking Christa up that way, he has completely changed me. As I sit on the couch, trembling with rage, I can barely recognize the person I have become.

The old Emma is gone for good. I hope he's ready to fight the new version of me. This version is not afraid to kill for survival.

I spend the next hours doing what he wants. I wipe away the tears and give him smiles I don't mean.

"You were right," I say after breakfast. "I *do* like that we're alone."

He reaches out his hands and pulls me from the chair and into his arms. "I'm glad you now see why I had to do it."

"Yes," I nod. "I get it now."

He kisses me hard on the lips and I kiss him right back, giving him the kiss of death.

The rest of the day, I pretend to be his wife, as I had planned. I show him the affection he craves in every way possible. I don't fight him once.

In the evening, he brings a portable hot plate to the kitchen from the basement. He had it down there all along while he forced my sister to cook over an open fire? What an ass.

I cook dinner while he lights the candles. He really believes that this fake romance is real.

As we eat, I watch the candlelight flickering on his face. When he smiles, I smile back. It's one of the hardest things I have ever done in my life.

"I love you, Emma, so much." He brings a glass of water to his mouth and takes a swig, his eyes never leaving my face.

I finish chewing before lying to him. "I love you too, Dax."

When dinner is over, he pulls me out of my chair and sweeps me off my feet. This time, when he lays me in bed, he doesn't handcuff me. But he locks the doors and windows, so there's still no way for me to get away.

13

When Dax wakes up in the morning, his cock is deep in my mouth, hardening as I suck on it. I've never been a great fan of blow jobs, but this is a matter of life and death. I'm willing to pay whatever price it takes to get our freedom back. Last night, it dawned on me that I can use his weakness to get what I want.

My eyes are closed, my hands moving up and down his shaft. I don't need to look at him to know he's watching me.

He grunts and stretches out his legs, placing his hand on my shoulder. "Look who's keeping her end of the bargain. This is a nice little treat." His voice is thick with sleep.

I'm glad to be occupied so he doesn't

expect a response from me. I continue to move my mouth up and down his hardness while circling it with my tongue at the same time.

"Yes. That's it, baby." He moves his hand to my head and pushes himself deeper into my mouth, hitting the back of my throat. I do my best to avoid gagging and tell myself it will all be over soon.

I continue pleasuring him until his body jerks and stiffens, and he comes into my mouth. I would've preferred to spit out his cum, but instead I swallow.

There's so much on the line right now. One little mistake and everything could blow up in my face. He can never know that I'm fooling him, that I have a plan.

Whatever happens, I cannot allow myself to be thrown into the dungeon. Not because of the snakes, but because time spent there would be wasted. Every second of my time should be spent working on my plan of escape.

He trusts me again, enough to keep the handcuffs off. I can't mess this up.

He's grinning from ear to ear as he pulls me to himself and kisses me. Minutes pass with him still holding me. For a split second, my body almost remembers how it used to be, when I loved him. But I shut the memories down before they cloud my mind.

"Come on, let's take a shower together." He gets up from the bed and takes me by the hand. Inside the shower, he washes my body, taking his time, paying attention to every part of me. When he gets to my vagina, I cringe inwardly. Shit. His dick is hard again.

What was the point of waking him up with a blow job? My intention had been to make him come so he wouldn't want to fuck me, at least for a while.

Thankfully, my fears don't materialize. He simply rinses off the soap he has spread across my skin, then moves on to my head to wash and massage my scalp.

I hold my breath, waiting for him to finish. Every time he touches my head I remember everything that happened on the yacht. When he shaved me, he didn't only steal my hair. He stole everything. My locks were a symbol of all the good things he destroyed in my life.

Soon he washes himself as well and steps out of the shower. He hands me a towel and takes one for himself. We get dressed in silence.

Instead of the dress I had been wearing, he gives me one of his white shirts. It looks like a mini dress on me.

"You make it look sexy," he says as he buttons it up.

Still in a good mood after what happened in bed, he makes us breakfast.

His good mood stays with him the rest of the day. Every chance he gets he touches my breast or my ass. He enjoys having me at his fingertips.

It's torture to carry a fake smile on my face the entire day while inside I'm coming undone. But it's what I've got to do. I don't even mind the cleaning, because now it has a purpose. Everything I'm doing now is for a reason. I'm determined that this will be the best performance of my life. It has to be.

The only hiccup is that his fear of me running away is still there. To prevent that from happening, when he's not watching me like a hawk, he locks me inside every room that I have to clean, only letting me out when I'm done. I appreciate the space.

Without him in the room, I have the opportunity to search in peace for objects that could prove useful to me later. Every cupboard and drawer I open could be hiding something that could aid in my escape—a toilet brush, a hanger, a pumice stone, anything. Since I can't take anything back with me to the bedroom I simply gather them in one place in each room to retrieve when I get the chance.

Once my work is done for the day, he asks me to take a break.

"You've been working all morning," he says. "Come and eat lunch. I cooked spaghetti."

Looks can be deceiving. From the outside, we look like any normal couple, enjoying a day together. A stranger would never guess that there's a darkness looming above us.

After lunch, Dax does a bit of work on the farm, tending to the horses, repairing the chicken coop, and other farm tasks that require his attention. Every time he works, he wants me to be near him, to keep him company. I don't mind following him around, except when he takes me to the stables near the shed that houses Christa.

While he tends to the horses, I strain my ears to listen for any kind of sound coming from the shed. Nothing.

Cold fingers of dread touch my spine, but I don't allow the fear to show on my face. He doesn't even glance at the shed. To him, it's as though my sister does not even exist.

Please God, let her be all right. I hope that the reason she's quiet is because she's sleeping. She won't be in there for long. I plan to carry out my plan within a day or two, if not sooner. Every second counts.

"How are you, my love?" Dax asks when we later sit by the lake that cuts through the property, watching ducks gliding over the sparkling water.

"Fine." I clasp my hands together in my lap. "I'm okay."

"I'm glad to hear that. By the way, how do you like farm life so far? Is it as hard as I warned you it would be?" He tosses a piece of bread into the water for the ducks to enjoy while Christa starves.

"It's a little hard," I say. It's best to keep my true thoughts and feelings to myself. "But I can handle it."

"Come on, you don't have to lie to me. I grew up on a farm. I know how much work it can be. It must be particularly hard for you, especially since you don't have most of the luxuries you were accustomed to."

"You're right. It takes a little getting used to." I pause for a long time. "Are there any other farms nearby?"

"Not really. This property is pretty isolated. That's what I liked about it. The closest thing is a gas station but it's quite a drive away."

Disappointment tears through me. How would we be able to make it to safety if there's no immediate place for us to hide or anyone to turn to for help?

I'm desperate to ask him where exactly we are, but I know he would not be happy about that. I keep my mouth shut and we feed the ducks in silence, with me wishing I could give the bread to Christa instead. I imagine her lying in the middle of the shed, curled up in a ball, broken by hunger and thirst.

I clear my throat. "Dax, don't you think we should give Christa some more water?" I know what the answer will be before I get it, but I had to try.

"No." His tone is sharp. "I already told you that she was not getting any more water than what I already gave her."

"Do you really want her to die?" I chew on my inner cheek. "There are other ways to get her out of the way. Death doesn't have to be the answer."

"There's no other way, my love." He takes my hand in his and squeezes. "You have to understand that this is the best decision for both of us. We have to learn to live with it. Just pretend she's gone already. That's what I'm doing."

"Are we ever going back to the city?" I ask, changing the subject.

"We don't need to. We have it pretty great here. If we run out of any supplies, my pilot will bring us more. We'll be happier without the city life, don't you think?"

"Yeah," I force a smile even though I'm

drowning in grief. "I guess so."

"That's my girl." He rewards me with a smile. "We have everything we need. We have each other. I plan to spend every moment of my life with you," he says, kissing my cheek.

"Me too."

"I love the sound of that." He gets up from the bench. "We should get back to the house. It will get dark soon." He pulls me to my feet and we hold hands on the way to the farmhouse.

He cooks dinner and tells me I will be his dessert. We've already had sex twice today and I'm not in the mood for more. It hurts just thinking about having him inside of me again.

I'm surprised when we get to bed that he doesn't actually make love to me. Instead, he undresses me and himself, then he lies next to me, his arms tight around my body, our bodies pressed against each other. He holds me until he falls asleep.

I try to move away from him, but he tightens his arms around me to keep me in place. Even asleep, he has so much power over me.

14

I'm locked inside the bathroom connected to our bedroom while Dax is in the room on the other side of the wall. He called it his office and I'm not allowed inside. He mentioned that he has some work to do and I should clean to occupy myself. He has been away for quite some time.

Even though every surface is clean, I continue to scrub. I'm glad he's not around me. He was by my side for most of the day and I was desperate to be alone. Being alone means not having sex with him, and I don't have to look in his eyes and lie to him.

Every time I tell him a lie, I fear I will be caught. So far, I've been lucky, but for how long? I can't handle it any longer. I already intend to carry out my plan before the day is over. But I'm afraid I might fail. That's why I needed to be alone so I can gather up the courage to act.

He told me that once I'm done I should call for him or knock on the door, so he can let me out. But I keep hesitating.

Feeling as though a weight is pushing down on my shoulders, I sink to the edge of the bathtub and drop my head into my hands. The headache I'd been carrying since morning is determined to torment me.

After counting to a hundred, I push myself to my feet and take a step toward the door. Then the sound of voices seeps through the wall. I know there's no one visiting us, so he must be talking on the phone and the other person is on speaker.

Seeing his phone or hearing him make a phone call always gives me hope. He has kept an open line to the outside world and soon I'll be able to get in touch with someone who can help me.

Curious about his conversation, I climb into the wet bathtub and press my ear against the wall. It still surprises me how thin these walls are. That's why I was able to hear Christa crying from her room.

"What the fuck is going on, Dax?" The voice that makes it through to my ears is deep and has a German accent attached to it. "Why are you not returning any of our calls?"

"I've been busy." Dax's voice sounds wary. He doesn't sound like he's in the mood for conversation.

"Sure you are. The killing spree must be going perfectly." There's a pause. "We know about everything you've been up to. What happened to reporting back to us?" The man sounds as though he's speaking through clenched teeth. "You're playing a risky game, man. You are getting out of hand. Kill the bitch and get it over and done with."

"No," Dax says louder than I'm sure he intended to be. "I can't kill this one."

"Why not? You've killed others, many others." The stranger's tone is coolly disapproving.

"I love her, all right? I love this one more than the others. She's my wife."

"And that's exactly the problem. When

you joined the club, we warned you not to bring your heart into the game. If you recall, that was rule number one."

"The damn club does not control me," Dax retorts. "I'm still my own person, I make my own rules."

"Not if you're one of us. As a member, you follow the rules or else we eliminate you."

As I listen to the words exchanged, alarm bells go off inside my head. I have a feeling I'm about to find out some of Dax's deepest, darkest secrets. It scares the hell out of me.

"What the fuck are you trying to say to me?" His voice is raw and dusty.

"I'm saying you have two choices here. All the members agree that you're putting the club at risk. Either you kill her, or we will destroy you."

Dax laughs out loud, but there's an obvious strain to the sound. "What will you do, kill me?"

"Eventually. But first we will destroy your reputation. All the secrets you're hiding will come out into the light."

"What secrets?"

"Come on, don't act stupid. We all know you didn't write that New York Times bestseller that took you to Hollywood. *Ragged Waves* is the title, am I right? I'm actually holding a copy in my hands right now."

In the silence that follows, I press my ear even harder against the wall, my heart pounding so hard it's difficult to hear.

"You thought we didn't know, didn't you?" It's the other man's turn to chuckle. "You're terrible at covering up your mess."

"You know nothing," Dax barks, but I catch the tremble at the edge of his words.

"That's where you're wrong, Mr. Hollywood. We also know you have way more to hide. When you joined the club, you only told us about one murder. How about the others? You didn't only kill your father. You killed the writer of the manuscript you stole. You—"

"Shut the fuck up." Dax's voice is so sharp it cuts through the wall and slams into my eardrums.

"Look, I'm calling to let you know that we're tired of covering your ass. When you joined, you were given one other simple rule to follow. One murder a year and nothing more. But you haven't followed that rule, have you?"

"I'm tired of you and everyone else telling me what to do. You know what, I'm out. So is my money."

"No, bro. It's not as simple as that. You've done too much damage to simply walk away. There are consequences to your irresponsible actions."

A long silence follows which makes me think Dax has ended the call, but he speaks again, his defeated voice cutting the silence. "What do you want me to do? How do you expect me to kill her?"

"Like you killed the rest. You're an expert. How about you make it look like a suicide? It shouldn't be hard. You already made everyone believe she's a junkie. Say she overdosed."

"No, fuck you and fuck them all. I'm not killing her."

I sink to the bottom of the bathtub, trembling and unable to believe what I heard. Dax is not the only monster out there. He's working with someone else, a whole club of monsters.

When their voices break through the wall again, I pull myself to my feet even though my knees are threatening to give way.

"You don't have to do it alone. You should've known that from the start. Kill her and we will get rid of her body for you. We will use our best resources if we have to. There are cops on the team ready to help you clean up this mess you've made," the man says. "But you have to make a quick decision. You have three days to kill her or we will come and kill you both." He clears his throat. "And while you're at it, kill the sister as well."

"How do you—"

"I already told you. We know everything about our members. Get the job done and call the headquarters."

The alarm bells inside my head are so loud now that I can no longer hear what they're saying. I sink back to the bottom of the bathtub and wrap my arms around my legs. But I snap out of my shock immediately because I know he will be back soon. I can't hear anyone talking which means he might have ended the call.

The moment I stand again, a wave of dizziness hits me. With the help of the basin, I climb out of the bathtub and take a few steps toward the door. But I stop myself from knocking, terrified of coming face to face with him. He's much more dangerous than I ever thought possible. The other man's words won't stop repeating in my head.

Dax lied to everyone in Hollywood. He's not the author of *Ragged Waves*. He murdered his way into the movie industry. The world will be shocked to find out he's both a liar and a murderer.

Of all the information I heard today, the most terrifying is that there are other monsters like him out there, people who kill one person a year, as though it's some kind of sick game they play. How many are there?

I need to pull myself together. He can't see me in this state, shaking and drenched with sweat. If he sees me now, he'll know immediately that something is off. He'll put two and two together.

If he ever finds out that I know, his decision to kill me will be so much easier.

That's if he hasn't already decided to do what the other man told him: to end my life right away.

Still dizzy, I turn away from the door and go to the sink to splash cold water on my face.

With water dripping from my chin, I clutch onto the edge of the sink, my fingers so tight that my knuckles whiten. Tears and water drip into the sink when I bend my head forward.

I slide my bottom lip between my teeth to stop it from trembling and force myself to hold it together. I have no choice now. I have to carry out my plan. The end has come. I have to kill him before he kills me and Christa.

The fear trickling through my veins drives me to fling open one of the cupboards where I hid some of the items I want to use.

My unsteady hand goes to a metal hanger I found under the cupboard, yesterday. Thinking quickly, I straighten it. I shudder when the sound of something crashing to the floor hits the wall, followed by curses flying all over the place.

I move even faster, lifting the shirt to wrap the hanger around my stomach. Then I sit on the edge of the tub and wait for him to come and get me. Hopefully he will not shoot me before I get a chance to act. But I think that would be too messy. It would be hard to call my death a suicide.

Or maybe he won't kill me. He might decide to ignore the other man's orders. Driven by his obsession, he might take me and run to another place where no one will find us.

Both scenarios terrify me. If he takes me away, I won't be able to see Christa again. She will die in the shed. No one will be able to find her in time.

When a door slams, I scramble to my feet. I can hear every footstep as he makes his way back to the room. My mind follows the sound all the way to the bathroom door. I can hear him breathing heavily as he stands on the other side. My own breathing is labored. But I'm ready for war.

My hands curl into fists at my sides as I mentally prepare myself to become like him. To become a killer.

15

The door to the bathroom is finally flung open. When our eyes lock, I hope he doesn't see through me to my thoughts. One little suspicion from his end and it's over for me.

Standing in the doorway with nostrils flared and neck corded, I know something has shifted inside him. He's furious. Is it with me or the man on the phone?

"Do you love me, Emma?" A dark chill coats the edge of his words. "Tell me the truth."

My body stiffens from the inside. On the outside, I do my best to stay calm.

I don't need to answer his question. He knows the answer. I've told him often enough on the yacht, but his twisted mind refuses to face reality.

I know what he's trying to do. He's trying to decide whether he should kill me or let me live. He wants me to make it easy for him to pull the trigger. If I want to live, I have to feed him lies again.

I part my lips to tell him the words he wants to hear. To my surprise, they refuse to leave my lips.

My mind is still spinning from what the caller revealed about Dax, that he was never the man I thought he was. He was a lie from the start.

My gaze searches his eyes. I only find lies there. I can't do it. I can't find it in me to tell him I love him, not even if I don't mean it. Not this time.

"Answer my damn question." He looks like a volcano on the verge of erupting. "The question is simple. Do you love me or not?" He takes a step toward me, his nails digging into his palms, his hands shaking.

I take one step back. "I don't. . . I don't get why you're asking. I already told you how I feel about you."

"Say it again. I want to hear the words."

His jaw is tight, his eyes boiling pools of fury.

I tilt my head back and cross my arms. "I'm tired, Dax. Let's talk about this later." I know my response will piss him off. It's all part of the plan. The time has come for me to put my plan into action sooner than I had planned. But I worked on this plan late into the night while he slept soundly next to me. I might fail and end up dead, but I might also succeed.

"Don't fuck with me, Emma." He charges forward. My breath catches when his hand closes around my neck. Air bursts from my lungs when he slams my back against the wall. "I'm having a really bad day. Don't make me do something I might regret."

"I—I—" It's hard to speak when I can barely breathe from his hands and the rope of fear wrapped around my neck.

I thought I was ready for this, but now I'm not so sure. What if he kills me now and I don't get a chance to carry out my plan?

"You what, Emma?" He brings his face close to mine. His spit lands on my skin.

"Love," I manage to croak. My hands clutch his, my fingers trying to unravel his before I lose my strength and my plan goes to hell.

"That's not enough." To both my relief and shock, he loosens his grip and shoves me away from him. "You hesitated."

With my hands around my neck, I gasp and cough, greedily snatching oxygen from the air. It's not enough. It doesn't matter how much I inhale; the oxygen will never be enough to fill my lungs.

The truth is, I stopped breathing weeks ago, when he kidnapped me. I'll only be able to breathe again when all this is over.

"Now what?" I ask, meeting his gaze without flinching, even though my bladder is loosening. "What will you do to me? Will you throw me into your dungeon?" I drop my hands to my sides and shrug. "Fine, go ahead."

"Maybe I should." His eyes narrow to glowing flints. "Maybe it's time for me to release the snakes." Before I can recover from his earlier attack, his hand shoots out again and grabs the back of my neck. His touch awakens the pain from the cigarette burn. "Let's go."

If he's surprised that I'm not fighting him, he doesn't show it. I have my reasons for not struggling. The last thing I need is for him to see the hanger around my stomach.

With each step I assure myself it will all be fine. Everything is working according to plan.

When we get to the door of the dungeon, I spin around to face him, fresh tears in my eyes. "No," I shake my head. "Please, don't. I'm sorry. I didn't mean—"

"Too little, too late." He unlocks the door and throws it open. When he shoves me inside, my arms are around my stomach to prevent the shirt from going up and revealing my weapon. I land on my knees. I keep my eyes away from the snakes underneath me and focus on the most dangerous one of all. This is it. I only have a few seconds to act before he slams the door shut. "Dax, I'm really sorry. Come here, please. Let me explain."

Just as I had planned, he charges into the room, his face a mask of rage. He can't stay away from me, in anger or lust. From his expression, I can tell that he has finally realized the truth.

"What's there to explain, huh? Do you want to explain all the lies you've been feeding me?" He comes closer, falling straight into my trap. "You've made a fool of me long enough. It ends today."

He hovers over me, his hands in thick fists at his sides, the knuckles white. "I gave you so many chances. I even kept your sister alive. I should've killed her a long time ago, but I knew how devastated you would be." His laughter chills my spine. "I was such an idiot. You're just like all the rest, a piece of shit."

I press my teeth together, force myself not to react yet. One mistake and I'll be dead.

"Why so quiet? Don't you have anything to say? Won't you tell me I'm wrong?" The murderous look in his eyes warns me we've reached the point of no return.

"Dax, please," I say quickly. "Don't kill me. You love me. You said so yourself."

"That's right," he shouts. "I love you. I've loved you from the moment I first laid eyes on you in your shitty little town.

That's why I gave you everything. I opened doors for you." He sucks in a shaky breath. "But it's over now. Is there anything you want to say before you die?"

"My sister. . . Please let her live."

"How many times do I have to repeat myself? I already told you the bitch is not leaving this farm alive. Neither will you." He starts to pace the room. It looks as though some of the snakes are following his movements.

It's amazing how I'm more terrified of him than the snakes.

"As soon as I'm done with you, I'm going straight to the shed to blow her brains out. That's if she's not dead already." He halts and taps his lips with a finger. "Even better, maybe I should set the damn place on fire and let her die a painful death. Either way, she'll be paying for your sins." He pinches the bridge of his nose. "Such a shame you won't get to say goodbye."

"It's me you want, Dax. She did nothing to you." I squeeze my eyes shut and gather up the courage to take the next step. I crawl toward him, looking up at him with pleading eyes. "Let her go. Spare her."

Someone is dying today, and it won't be me. It won't be Christa either if she's still alive. God, I hope she's still alive. We have too much to live for.

I need my life and freedom back. I need to avenge the people he has wronged, hurt, or killed. The lives of his future victims are in my hands. He has destroyed enough lives. The time has come to end this madness once and for all.

16

Whatever I do, I can't look away from his eyes. This is the moment I've been waiting for. I have to make it work.

My breath shakes as I crawl across the floor toward him.

"Stay where you are. What the fuck do you think you're doing?" He takes a few steps in the direction of the door.

"Give me another chance, please. Let me prove myself to you." I do not have to force pain into my voice because it's already there. It's real. "Don't do this to me, Dax. You don't want to kill me."

"Damn right. I don't want to kill you." He shakes his head. "But sometimes we have to do things we don't want. I'm doing this because I love you so damn much."

He shoves a hand into his hair. "But you have betrayed me over and over again. You've run out of chances, sweetheart."

He takes another step toward the door, away from me. My stomach twists as my chance of escape starts to slip through my fingers. Left with no choice and no more time, I spring to my feet and throw myself at his feet, holding tight to his legs so he doesn't move. "I don't want to die." My eyes well up with tears. My fear of death is real. I don't doubt for one second that if Dax leaves this room, he will push the switch that will end my life.

"It's over. I'm done with you." He tries to shake me off, but I hold on. It's a matter of life and death. He tries once more to push me away. This time he succeeds but loses his balance. He stumbles backward, his back hitting the wall next to the door.

I make it to him before he can recover, taking hold of his legs again, crawling my way up. "No, it's not over, baby," I choke on my tears. "I do love you, Dax. I love you so much. Let me show you one more time."

He looks down at me, his eyes a dark shade of amber. Like mine, they're shining with tears.

Dax Pierce is crying. He lied about a lot of things in his life, but the truth is, he does love me. Only not in the way I want to be loved. His love hurts way too much.

"You mean that?" He wipes the tears from his cheek with the back of his hand.

He looks so weak, like a little boy. Deep down he wants to be needed, to be loved. But I cannot find it in me to feel sorry for him. I don't even know who he is. He's a complete stranger to me.

"I mean it with all my heart." My lips tremble as I speak. "I never stopped loving you. You're the one for me. But you hurt me, Dax." I continue to crawl up his legs. "But it doesn't have to be like that anymore. We can begin again, you and me. Let me prove my love to you."

He doesn't push me away when I tug his hands until he's on the floor with me. I place myself between his legs.

He doesn't move a muscle as I unzip his pants and push my hand inside. He's already hard. How can he be turned on in a situation like this? I'm his weakness. This weakness will be his downfall.

He presses the palms of his hand behind him on the wall as though he's trying to hold on, to keep from falling into my arms. Too late. I've got him right where I want him.

"It's okay," I whisper. "I'm here. I want to prove to you that you're the only man I ever want. You don't want us to really be over. You were right all along. We're meant to be together."

He opens his mouth to speak, but nothing comes out. More tears trickle down his cheeks.

Here he was pretending to be a strong man when he's nothing but a little boy desperate for love and affection. It was the boy inside who believed the lies I told him, who believed me when I said I loved him.

Suddenly he knocks the back of his head against the wall behind him and shakes his head. The dangerous man returns. "Back off," he growls. He plants his hands on my shoulders to push me away again, but there's no way I'm letting go. Not when I've come this far, not when I've seen the fragile side to him.

"You don't want that." I kiss his lips. "Let me make you feel good. I can make it all better, baby. You will love it, I promise." With a small smile I pull out his dick and cover it with my mouth. I don't give him a chance to say no.

A defeated groan escapes him and the anger on his face is quickly replaced by lust.

I suck him until his body loses strength and he's barely able to keep his head upright. Even when my jaw starts to ache, I don't stop. There's only one way to get what I want. His dick is my weapon.

I only stop when I know he's about to come. My gaze on his face, I remove his penis from my mouth. "Should I continue? Is this what you want?"

"Don't fucking stop. Don't. . ." Whatever more he wanted to say dies on his lips when I slide him back into my mouth, flicking my tongue as I go, pushing him even deeper.

I suck harder, my hands moving faster around the bottom of his shaft.

The moment I realize I'm completely in

control, and he's far gone, I sink my teeth into his flesh so fast and so hard he doesn't see it coming.

The guttural roar that bursts from him bounces off the walls and deafens my ears momentarily.

He grabs my head and tries to push me away, but I'm determined to end this game my way. I bite until I taste blood. As soon as I let go, I don't waste time.

While his hands are on his injured penis, I jump to my feet. He's already down and I didn't even need to use the hanger.

Before I can distance myself from him, one of his hands shoots out and grabs my ankle. I manage to kick him away and stumble to the door.

"Get back here, you bitch. Where the fuck do you think you're going?"

I look back once to see him panting, his hands still around his cock, his face red with pain and anger.

A tiny glow spreads through my chest. I can't stay long enough to revel in it. It's time to run to the finish line. It's only a matter of time before he pushes through the pain and comes after me.

When he starts to crawl toward me, I grab the handle and yank open the door, burst out of the room, and slam it shut behind me. Since he was so stupid to leave the key in the lock, he'll pay a high price. Without a moment's hesitation, I lock him inside his dungeon.

Another roar comes from the other side, the sound so satisfying it sends a wave of pleasure sweeping through my body. I place a hand on my neck, suddenly sick from the taste of his blood. I spit out what I can and wipe my lips with the back of my hand. Then I remove the hanger and toss it to the floor. I no longer need it.

But it's not over yet. I need to carry out the entire plan.

I consider removing the key from the keyhole, but that would be too risky. What if he has another key inside his pocket? I'm not about to find out.

I can hear him scratching the other side of the door and hammering against it. "You fucking cunt. Open the damn door."

My heart is racing so fast that I need to catch my breath before taking the next step. What I'm about to do is completely outside my comfort zone.

I slump forward, my hands on my knees and pull air into my lungs. The exhaustion that had been building up for days now finally catches up with me. My body is telling me to quit, to sink to the floor and get some rest. I do crumple to the floor, but I'm not about to give up. Not when I'm this close.

You can do this, Emma.

I inhale sharply, then crawl to the final destination. Even with him trapped inside, my fear of him still paralyses me.

I notice the metal switch immediately, next to the tiny window he had watched us from. There's another one next to it.

A weight settles on my chest when sudden silence falls around me. Why is he quiet? Is there another way for him to get out?

I grit my teeth and use every ounce of energy left in my body to pull myself up the wall, toward the switches. My nails scratch against the hard surface, tearing away the paint. One of them breaks, but I don't care. Only one thing matters to me right now. An image of Christa's broken face flickers in my mind.

I need to save her. Failure is not an option.

17

I peer through the small window, still unable to believe I have the upper hand now, that I'm on the other side.

I'd hoped for this day, prayed it would come, but at the back of my mind I was worried I would never win against him.

My eyes blur with tears of relief. I can't even describe the feeling of watching him broken for once.

Since he has moved to the center of the room, I can see him clearly, surrounded by his snakes. Both his hands are clutching his crotch. I must have hurt him badly; he can't even put his penis back in his pants. I can see it through his fingers.

Now he knows how it feels to hurt. Sadly for him, I'm not done with him yet. I will hurt him more than he hurt me, more than he hurt anyone before me.

Since he doesn't seem like a threat at the moment, I place both my hands flat against the glass. My lips curl into a smile of victory. It's goodbye.

Maybe I should go and call the cops so they can take over, but I don't trust him not to escape. He built the dungeon. He might find a way out.

No way. I have to handle this myself.

I wait until he looks up and our eyes meet. "It's over," I mouth.

He crawls across the floor to the place below the window. I can no longer see him completely, but I know what he's doing. He's trying to pull himself up, to get closer to me. It's an effort that fails. Seconds later, he's lying flat on his back.

Even though his body is broken, his eyes are a different story. As he scrambles to a seated position, I watch them smolder with fire.

His eyes still on me, he lifts a hand and draws a finger across his throat. Even behind closed doors, inside a room full of deadly creatures, he still believes he has the upper hand. He probably thinks I don't have the guts to finish this game. It baffles me that a person in such a weakened state can still afford to be such an asshole.

I look to the levers on my side, then back at him, my blood boiling.

"Don't you dare, you fucking whore," he shouts, baring his teeth. "Don't you fucking dare."

Now he's pissing me off. It's time to teach him a lesson. "Watch me." I raise my hand to the switch labeled "floor opening". The second switch is labeled "electric fence".

I place a finger on the switch. It's cool against my skin. "This fucking whore is the last person you'll ever see," I say.

Holding onto the wall for balance and support, I flick the switch.

Bloody hell. He wasn't kidding. Everything is happening exactly as he said it would. I watch in amazement as on one end a part of the glass lifts a few inches from the ground and slides to the side to create an opening for the snakes to escape.

I'm betting when he built the room, he never thought he'd be building his own grave.

I watch with bated breath as the snakes slither through the opening, fangs bared.

Since he's close to the opening, they get to him pretty fast. I can see he wants to move away, but fear has rooted him to the spot.

I'm unable to look away as the reptiles get ready to take revenge on the man that kept them trapped beneath the glass, and maybe even starved them.

Dax's eyes widen in panic as more and more snakes slither out. It's hard to count them. Maybe ten are headed his way. Many more are still under the glass, but I doubt they will be for long.

He tries to stand again, but fear stops him from standing upright. Soon his legs quit on him and he crumples back to the floor. While he's down and unable to move, his face white as a sheet, a moss green snake slithers onto his body and sinks its fangs into his flesh. Others follow.

The screams that burst out of him hit the walls and bounce off.

In his own personal hell, his gaze briefly moves to mine but only for a few seconds before he closes his eyes. One of the larger snakes raises its head moments before it strikes his cheek like a dart aiming at its target. Another attacks his penis.

The guttural scream that pours out of his mouth as he tries to push away the snake attached to his crotch are almost painful to hear. I'm in shock at the brutality in front of me.

It makes me sick to think the person in there could have been me, that Dax could have been the one standing on this side, watching.

He had unleashed a snake on his father that killed him. Now he's dying from snakebite as well. I bet he didn't see that coming.

"Good night, Dax Pierce," I call out, a slight crack in my voice. "Don't worry, your memory will live on, but not in a good way. I'll be sure to pass on the news that you didn't write the novel you claimed was yours. You piece of scum."

Amidst all the blood smeared on his face, I watch his undamaged eye open, but not for long. It's over. His body is trembling, and blood is pouring from every surface. I know he heard me, and he was shocked that I know the truth.

Still determined to destroy him, I consider running into the kitchen to get something to set fire to the farmhouse with, but I stop myself when it hits me that the snakes in the dungeon are as innocent as I am. They, too, are his victims. They don't deserve to die with him. They did their job and, for that, they get to live.

No point in setting fire to the place anyway. There's no way he can escape, no way he can live through this.

The relief is so intense that it's overwhelming me to the point where I sink to the floor, my head on my knees. Hot tears fill my eyes and drip onto the floor. Sobs break through my body.

I allow myself to cry for a moment, then I stand again to look through the window. In the bloody mess, I can barely recognize him. But I can't look away, not yet. I need to make sure he's completely gone, that he won't come back to hurt me. I have to make sure that whatever remains of him will only be inside my head.

His body shakes for a while, then it goes

limp. The snakes continue to wrap themselves around his limbs, to revel in the taste of his blood.

It's done. It's really over. Watching him lying there helpless, I remember the person who gave me the strength to stand up to him. Christa.

I put one foot forward and stumble through the hallway, my body in pain.

I'm about to go on the search for the keys to his truck, when I remember that every time he drove it, he never removed them from the ignition. I also know that the key to the shed is on the same key ring. There's nothing stopping me from going to Christa, but I need something else.

I run to the room he said was his office. I don't even need to enter completely to see the cell phone. It's right there on the floor next to the door, with a shattered screen. He must have flung it there after his phone call with the person who threatened him. I don't have time to fix it right now. I need to get to Christa and make sure she's okay, so I run out of the house.

On my way out, I fall a couple of times,

but an image of my sister lying lifeless inside the shed forces me to get back to my feet.

I don't stop until I get to the truck and jump behind the wheel. After a few tries, I manage to bring the vehicle to life. I drive like a maniac through the narrow, potholed, dirt road headed to the stables. Every second counts.

Please, God, don't let it be too late.

I find her lying on her back, unmoving, surrounded by the stench of urine.

My breath solidifies in my lungs as I try to shake her awake. She doesn't respond. My shaking hands feel for a pulse. I find it, but it's weak. I need to get her to the hospital as fast as possible.

"Christa, sweetie, it's over," I say with tears in my voice.

I don't hear the sound of her voice, but I notice a twitch of her cracked lips. I almost collapse with relief.

"That's good, sweetheart. Please hang in there. I'll get you out of here."

It's a struggle to get her to the truck, but even with the lack of energy, I'm fueled by my desperation to save her. I half carry and half drag her to the vehicle until I succeed.

I want to drive off right away, but then I remember the fence. I might need to turn off the electricity.

The last place I ever want to set foot in again is the farmhouse, but it has to be done. My fingers are clenched at my sides as I tear through the house, still feeling the fear he had implanted so deep into my heart. Before I flick the "fence" switch, I glance into the dungeon.

Blood drains from my face when I don't see him. He's not where I left him. The only hint he was there, is the blood on the glass and the snakes. Panic is about to arrest me, but I notice a bloody, swollen foot close to the place that's not completely visible from the window. I let out a relieved breath.

I guess he wasn't dead when I left. He must have been trying to get to the door but failed.

I don't waste any more time. I flick the switch, then run to the kitchen to grab two bottles of water.

I storm from the house again. This time I don't look back.

As I run toward my freedom, my stomach is still rock hard with nerves. In some way I'm still afraid something could go wrong. Even though I know there's no way he's still alive, another part of me is finding it hard to believe he's not immortal.

I push the truck as fast as it would go and don't even stop at the gate. I'm pretty sure it's locked and have no idea where the keys are. I'm not going back there. So I drive right through it, grateful it's one of those weak gates.

"Christa, please, talk to me." I glance at my sister from time to time, my hands sweaty on the steering wheel.

Her head is lolling from side to side and bouncing off her chest. She's showing signs of life, but she's so weak I'm afraid she might not make it.

Once I'm sure we're a safe distance away from the farmhouse and the devil himself, I stop the truck and give her water. She's too weak to even drink, but I do my best to make sure she takes at least a few drops.

Back behind the wheel, I pray it's not too late, that I have not caused my sister's death.

18

I finally stop again at the side of the road. I have to get Christa to drink more water. I try not to think of the worst. She can't die when we've come this far.

I force more water into her mouth. This time she drinks a little before her head dips to the side again. She can't even open her eyes.

I have no idea how long we've been driving. It feels like forever. Dax was right that this place is completely isolated. But he had mentioned something about a gas station and that's what I'm searching for. But what if it's such a great distance away that we don't make it in time for someone to save Christa?

I glance back at the road we had come.

My chest tightens when I still don't see a single car in sight.

"Sweetheart, please open your eyes for me. It's over. He's gone. He can no longer hurt us." I cradle her head and press my forehead to hers. I refuse to let her go. "I need you to fight, okay?"

When I pull away again, I watch her lips move more than they did before. A good enough sign of life.

"It's all right," I say, smiling through my tears. "You're going to be fine." I kill a sob and give her more water, then pour some on my hand. I drench her face with it to cool her down.

Back behind the wheel, I pick up Dax's phone from the dashboard where I had put it before.

Shit. As I gaze at the phone, the same disappointment that had hit me hard at the yacht, when I tried to call for help, returns. It's not switching on. I don't even know whether it's from a dead battery or from when Dax threw it.

"It's fine," I say, trying to assure myself. "We'll find someone who can help us."

Christa doesn't respond. She looks as

though she's sleeping. God, I hope she's sleeping.

I start the truck again. This time I push way past the speed limit. It's a matter of life and death and there are no other cars on the road I could be a danger to.

I'm about to give up hope of ever finding anyone, when I catch the glare of glass coming from the distance. The closer I come, the more it's confirmed to me that this is the gas station Dax was talking about.

The tears return to my eyes as I drive even faster toward our rescue.

A man with a long, gray beard and matching mustache is standing on the side of the road, smoking a cigarette.

When he sees our truck approach, he tosses the cigarette to the ground and crushes it with the toe of his shoe. He lifts his hand to shield his eyes, so he can see better through the bright sunlight. If he's the owner of the gas station, he must not see many people coming his way. He must be curious who we are. Or maybe he recognizes the truck.

I stop the truck so suddenly that

Christa's head bounces off the headrest before hitting it again.

"I'm sorry, sis." I squeeze her hand. "Someone is going to help us."

I almost fall from the truck as I get out too fast. Then I sway toward him, waving my hands as though I'm still a distance away. "Sir, I need your help, please. My sister—" I inhale a sharp breath. "My sister needs medical attention. Do you have a phone, please?"

The man watches me suspiciously for a long time, as though trying to figure out whether I'm a threat to him.

For goodness sake, do I look like a threat? I don't even need to look in the mirror to know I'm a complete mess.

The man pushes a hand into his pocket. I think he will bring out the phone, but instead his fingers emerge with a piece of gum, which he takes his time unwrapping before popping it into his mouth.

"If you don't help us, my sister will die in that truck." I point to the truck with a shaking finger. "Do you want to carry that on your conscience?"

"Who are you?" His voice is deep and

dusty.

I don't even know why that matters right now. There's a woman dying and he's not jumping in to help her. What's wrong with people?

"My name is Emma Stanton."

The man spits out his gum and his eyes widen at me. "The kidnapped actress?" He laughs. "You're shitting me."

"I'm not. . . I'm really not shitting you. I am Emma Stanton and I'm begging you to help my sister."

He frowns. "You don't look like her."

"That's because I went through fucking hell." I push the words through gritted teeth. "I was kidnapped by a madman. Will you help us or not?"

"Will you give me an autograph?" He winks.

"Yes, whatever you want. Please help."

He finally pulls out his phone and dials 911, his eyes still on me as though he can't believe I'm real. While on the phone, he moves toward the truck. I'm guessing the person on the other end is asking him questions about the state of Christa.

From his conversation, I gather that we

are in a town called Stonebay, Texas. I've never even heard of the place before.

"They're on their way," he says and pulls the phone away from his ear.

"Thank you." I wipe away my tears. "Thank you so much."

In the time we spend together, I learn that the man's name is Cory Brookins.

His demeanor completely changes when I give him the autograph I promised. I can only imagine how popular being in possession of my autograph will make him. It doesn't matter to me. The most important thing is that he saved us. I can't thank him enough, but when he offers to take Christa out of the truck and into his shop, I refuse.

After everything we have experienced at the hands of a man, I'm wary of being inside a room with someone we don't know.

He doesn't seem to mind. Instead, he brings out a plastic lawn chair and helps Christa onto it.

As soon as the sounds of sirens in the distance reach my ears, something shifts inside my body. Suddenly, every ounce of energy left in me melts away and I find myself falling, my legs completely giving way. Cory catches me before I hit the ground. In his arms, I close my eyes as darkness pulls me under.

When I wake up, we're inside an ambulance, my stretcher next to Christa's. Both our faces are covered by oxygen masks.

I remove my mask and a middle-aged female EMT with extremely long lashes and dark, oval eyes, smiles at me. "How are you feeling?"

"Tired," I say. My mouth feels dry. "How's my sister?"

"She's stable. She was dehydrated and she's been in shock. But I think she'll pull through. So will you." She places a hand on my forehead.

I nod. "Thank God." I don't care about me right now. Christa is my priority. As I watch her, tears seep from the corners of my eyes.

"I hope you don't mind, but the police are waiting at the hospital to talk to you."

"That's fine. I'll speak to them." I hesitate. "He wanted to kill us."

The woman looks at me confused. Clearly, she doesn't know most of the story. It doesn't stop me from blurting everything out, everything that had happened.

"He killed so many people." My eyes well up again.

"You were brave to get away from him," the woman says, tears in her eyes.

I close my own eyes again, feeling exhausted. Now that I'm on my way to freedom, I allow myself to relax. I give my body permission to let go completely.

19

I wake up feeling groggy and a bit disoriented. I have no idea how long I've been asleep. It feels like several hours.

In the first few seconds of wakefulness, my body automatically tenses, thinking I'm back on the farm. Then I remember what happened and feel myself sink into the mattress, overcome with relief.

My eyes feel heavy as I look around me without moving my head much because the headache lurking at the back of my skull won't let me. The bright lights in the white-washed room don't help.

I blink several times until my eyes get comfortable. It feels as though I had been trapped inside a dark room for days and now I have to adjust to the brightness.

I finally turn my head completely to the side, so I get a better view of one side of the room.

When I try to sit up, a female voice discourages me from doing so.

"Don't tire yourself out." A blonde nurse of about my age nears my bed and looks down at me with kindness. "How do you feel?" She has the whitest teeth I have ever seen on anyone and dimples that make her look younger than I think she is.

"How long have I been sleeping?" I ask the most important question to me at the moment.

"Just a couple of hours. But you're doing great. You were exhausted, which is understandable after everything you went through."

The EMT I talked to inside the ambulance must have passed on the news.

The nurse's words trigger something inside me that opens the door to the memories of what happened. The image of Dax sprawled on the dungeon glass floor with snakes on his body fills my mind. Then I remember Christa and how lifeless she had looked on the floor of the shed.

"My sister? Where's my sister?" A wave of panic rushes through me. I try to sit up again.

The nurse places a gentle hand on my shoulder. "Don't worry. She's fine now."

My eyes widen and my mouth goes dry. "What happened?" I had detected a slight hesitation in her voice. "Is she really fine?"

"She was dehydrated, and she showed some immediate Post-Traumatic Stress Disorder symptoms, but she's doing okay now. You're both going to be fine. But you will be monitored closely. Should anything change for the worse, you will be flown to a larger hospital in Dallas immediately."

The door opens and this time when I sit up, the nurse does not stop me. She's distracted by the sudden flurry of activity on the other side of the window that stands between my room and the hallway. The three pairs of eyes peering through the glass are police officers.

Another one of them stops in the doorway. "Miss Stanton, I'm Officer Garland from the Stonebay Police Department. May I come in? I would like to ask you a few questions, if you don't mind." The police officer has a thick, black beard with a gray stripe down the middle, and small, intense dark eyes.

"That's not a good idea, Jim," the nurse says. "Miss Stanton needs to rest."

They must know each other, which is not surprising in a small town.

I lift a hand from the bed sheet and give her a weak smile. "It's all right."

The officer will not be the only one with questions. Besides, they might need me to tell them where to find Dax's corpse.

"Fine," the nurse says and glances at me. "If he wears you out, ring the bell next to your bed." She leaves the room and the officer takes her place next to my bed. He lowers himself into the empty chair. The feet of the chair scrape the floor when he inches closer.

I bunch my hands into fists to stop them from shaking. Even though there will be enough evidence to prove what Dax did to me and Christa, a part of me cannot help but be terrified that the cops will think I'm a murderer, that they will not believe I did what I did out of self-defense.

"Thank you for your time, Miss Stanton. I won't be long." The way he's looking at me, with wide eyes and a big crooked smile, makes me remember who I was for a brief time in my life, a famous Hollywood actress. He's clearly star-struck in my presence. But he does his best to remain calm and professional during the questioning. "Mr. Brookins filled us in on your story, but it would be nice to hear your story straight from you."

I frown. "Who's Mr. Brookins?"

"The man who called 911. The owner of—"

"Right, yeah, I remember him. I told him what happened while we waited for help." I clutch my chest. "He's dead. Dax Pierce is dead." I squeeze my eyes shut and open them again slowly. I wish I could wipe the image of him from my mind. "It was self-defense. He was going to kill me. . . me and my sister."

"We know that. We found the farm where he held both of you hostage. There were cameras."

"So you saw everything?" I'm not surprised there were cameras on the farm.

"Yes, pretty much everything." He moves his gaze to the window for a moment as though he can't bear to even think about the horrors I went through. When he looks back at me, his eyes are warm and kind. "I'm so sorry for what you went through, Miss Stanton. You were brave to do what you did."

"Thank you." I wipe the moisture from my eyes and tell him the whole story from Hollywood to Stonebay, filling in the blanks in his mind.

Word by word I reveal all the layers of Dax Pierce. Going back to the horror of everything that had happened, there are times I need to take breaks, and he pours me a glass of water from a jug on the table.

By the time I'm done, I'm exhausted and his eyes are round with shock.

The questions after I'm finished telling my story take longer than he promised it would.

Finally, I tell him that I'm tired, but I'm open to questioning later. He respects that and thanks me.

He pushes himself to his feet and walks

to the door. Before he steps out, I call his name.

"There's something else," I say, biting my lip. "It might be important."

He turns around. His face is still pale with shock. "Everything is important at this point."

I tell him about the phone call I overheard while in the bathroom, that there are more people like Dax out there, dangerous people who kill like it's a game.

It's clearly new information to the officer because he returns into the room and starts jotting down my words. Maybe Dax's office didn't have cameras.

Since I don't have much more to tell him about the person I heard Dax talking to or the club he had been referring to, Officer Garland soon leaves, saying I gave him enough to work with.

When he's gone, a disturbing thought crawls to the forefront of my mind. What if the officer was one of the dirty cops? The man who was on the phone with Dax had mentioned that there were cops on their team ready to help Dax clean up his mess.

I force the thought from my mind. I won't make myself go crazy. I'm safe now.

When the nurse comes back to the room, I ask to make a phone call. She brings me a cell phone, which I use to call Curtis. The phone call goes straight to voicemail. I'm disappointed when I end the call and give the phone back.

"Can I see my sister?"

"She's sleeping right now. But you can see her later, after breakfast."

"I need to see her now." My lips are trembling. "She needs me, even if she's sleeping." I don't care if she doesn't speak to me. I want to make sure she's really all right, to see her with my own eyes.

"I understand." She touches my shoulder. "I'll take you to her."

The nurse wheels me to Christa's room. The distance is longer than I thought it would be. My dizziness makes us stop and I can tell the nurse wants to take me back to my room, but she doesn't say anything.

Outside Christa's room, I gaze through the open door. For a moment I simply watch her sleeping, her chest rising and falling. Warmth spreads through my chest.

My sister is alive. I saved her.

"Can I go in?"

"Of course. But try not to wake her." The nurse guides me into the room and helps me settle into the chair next to the bed. Even though Christa is hooked to some machines, there's color in her face and her lips. She looks better than she did when I rescued her.

I force my mind not to remember how I found her, how terrified I was that she wouldn't make it. My stomach still cramps up at the thought that I came close to losing her.

My eyes are burning as I cover my face with my hands.

"Don't you dare blame yourself, sis."

I look up. Through my blurry gaze, I notice a soft smile on her face. Joy bubbles up in my chest. She's back. "How can I not blame myself," I manage, choking up. "I did this to you."

"No." She shakes her head. "It wasn't you. How could you have known he was a monster?"

"But I should have listened to you, at the start. I shouldn't have chased fame." I grab her hand and hold on tight. "But it's over now. He can't hurt us anymore. I killed him, Christa. I unleashed the snakes on him."

"I knew you would find a way to save us. You did what you had to do." Her own eyes fill with tears. "You saved my life. So no more blaming yourself, okay? We're safe now. That's all. . . that's all that matters." She squeezes her eyes shut. Tears trickle down the sides of her face. "I was so scared for you, sis. I thought—"

"I thought he'd kill us both." I draw in a shaky breath. "I would never have been able to forgive myself if something happened to you. I'm sorry he treated you like a slave."

"As your big sister, I'm telling you to stop blaming yourself. Let's just look forward, okay?"

It takes me a long time to respond but finally I nod. I lift her hand to my lips and press a kiss on her skin.

"Are you all right?" Worry clouds her eyes. She knows I went through so much more than she was able to witness. She can sense how deep the wounds on my heart are.

"One day I will be. Right now, I'm just happy you're safe."

I give her a kiss on the cheek, then the nurse takes me back to my room for a round of tests. After we're done, I sink into the bed. I can finally breathe again.

After breakfast, I call Curtis again but I'm still unable to reach him. I leave a message telling him I've escaped and he can reach me at the hospital.

Two FBI agents show up to talk to me between breakfast and lunch. They explain that they will be the ones questioning me now and not the local police since Dax had taken me over state lines. They look legit so I tell them what I told the officer.

After they leave, I tell one of the doctors that I no longer want to be questioned. I also tell him to keep hospital employees from sneaking in for autographs. I'm desperate for some rest.

Finally alone, I lean back on the bed and turn on the small TV in time to see a local news station exploding with my story. It feels unreal to see snapshots of the farmhouse that has been my jail. Dax is being labeled a monster. I'm not even sure anymore whether that's the right title for him. He was so much worse. It's incredible how much information the press can capture within only a few hours.

As I watch the story unfold, my body clenches up again as though I'm back there.

I can't watch anymore. It's too painful. I turn off the TV again and close my eyes to shut out the painful images. I can't bear to even see his face on the screen.

20

My eyes open when the door opens. Happiness blooms inside my chest at the sight of him rushing into the room. While I have changed both physically and emotionally, he's the same man I left behind when I visited hell, but the spark that used to light up his blue bedroom eyes has died, and his face is a touch more serious than it used to be. But it's him. I never thought I'd see him again.

"Curtis," I say breathless. "My God, you're here."

For a moment he stops a few steps from the bed, studying me with broken eyes. He takes another step forward, then another. "Of course I'm here. As soon as I heard, I got on a plane. Jesus, are you okay?"

I don't answer as tears spring to my eyes. I sit up in bed and stretch out my arms. "Hug me, please."

He nods and comes to fold me in his arms. "You're alive." His voice is hoarse with tears. "I thought. . . God, I thought I would never see you." He pulls back to look at my face.

As his gaze takes me in, a wave of humiliation sweeps up my neck. "He shaved off my hair." I blink away tears. "He made me ugly."

"No." He places a thumb on my cheek to wipe away my tears. "He could never do that. You're as beautiful as the last time I saw you."

I want to believe his words badly, but right now I can't because I still feel the effects of Dax.

I allow him to pull me into another hug. For a few heartbeats, we hold each other in a silence that's only broken by our sobs. For the first time since Dax stole me, the knot in my stomach unravels and warmth spreads through my body, melting away some of the remaining pain.

In Curtis's arms, I notice how different

my feelings for him are now, but this is not the time or place to give thought to that. With what I'm going through, romance is the last thing on my mind. I'm happy to have my friend here. The next few days, months or maybe even years will be dedicated to finding myself and healing.

Curtis stays with me for a while, but when I try to tell him what happened, he's unable to hear it. He tells me he heard most of it already on the news and he doesn't want me to torture myself. So most of our time is spent in silence, in gratitude. With him by my side, I feel safe and grateful to have him as someone I can trust.

"Emma," he says finally. "I want you to know that I did everything to find you. I'm so sorry I failed." His face crumples with disappointment.

"Hey, don't do that." I squeeze his hand. "You're here now. And I'm alive."

We hug again but move apart when a doctor I haven't met yet steps into the room.

"I'm Dr. Daniels." He stretches out his hand to shake mine. "How are you feeling,

Miss Stanton?"

"I'm okay. . . tired." I feel like I've been run over by a truck and survived.

"Can we talk alone?" He glances at Curtis.

I frown. "Is everything all right, doctor?"

Dr. Daniels gazes at the clipboard in his hands. "Are you sure you don't want to talk in private?"

"No." I smile at Curtis. "This man is my agent and best friend. I want him to be here." The truth is, I'm a little terrified of what the doctor wants to tell me. I don't want to be alone.

"All right." He smiles. One of his teeth is slightly crooked. "I have your test results. Everything looks great, but there's something you should know." When he hesitates to continue, I cut in.

"Whatever it is, I can handle it." I've handled so much worse already. I can't imagine anything topping what I have gone through.

"We discovered that you're pregnant, Miss Stanton."

A gasp bursts from my lips and blood

drains from my face. I'm suddenly warm and cold at the same time. "How. . . No. Are you sure? I mean, I was pregnant. I told the nurse. But Dax, he made me take an abortion pill."

The doctor is silent for a moment. "Looks like it didn't work."

"But how's that possible?" I don't even look at Curtis, but I can feel his own shock cutting through the air. "I was bleeding."

"Some pregnancies survive the abortion pill. It could be that it wasn't administered properly."

Silence falls in the room and the only thing I can hear is my pounding heart, the blood rushing in my ears. I'm pulling in several deep breaths, one after the other to calm myself down, but it's not helping.

"Miss Stanton, are you okay?" the doctor asks.

"I don't know." I reach for my half empty glass of water and down the liquid. It's hard to hold the glass with my shaking hands, so I put it back down. "It's okay," I say. "It's. . . it's a bit of a shock, that's all." I swallow hard. "Thank you for letting me know, doctor."

"Of course." He gives me a kind smile.

I can't believe I'm still pregnant, after I had grieved my baby. I hated Dax for killing my baby before I had a chance to make a decision on whether I wanted to be a mother.

I place a hand on my stomach and keep it there, my eyes closed. "It's a miracle," I say softly. "It's a miracle."

"Yes, it is," the doctor agrees. He waits for me to open my eyes again and tells me he has other patients to see and will be back later.

"Are you okay?" Curtis asks when we're alone again. His already deep voice is even deeper. I can see he's also trying to contain the shock of what he heard. He doesn't reach out to touch or comfort me. I guess he doesn't know how to react in this situation. Maybe I should have agreed to talk to the doctor alone.

"I'm not really sure." I bite down on my lip. "But I think I want to keep it—the baby."

"Are you sure about that?" Curtis asks cautiously.

"I think I am." A trembling smile creeps

up on my face. "I think I have to." This baby survived trauma and it's still here, refusing to leave me. Right now, I'm not even thinking of it as the child of a murderer, just my baby. My innocent, miracle baby. I won't be alone after all. "I hated Dax with everything in me. But the baby is innocent."

Curtis blows out a breath and places his hand on my back. "You are one of the bravest women I have ever met."

"I'm not being brave. I'm only doing what my heart is telling me to." It will be a challenge to raise my child without remembering the horrors of the past, but I'll do it.

"Whatever you need, I'll be here. I'll support you in every way I can."

"As a friend." I need to say it. "Only as a friend, Curtis."

In this moment I cannot promise anything to anyone. The only promise I have is to my unborn child. I promise my baby that I'll do my best to heal so I can be a good mom. Thank God I have several months to get used to the idea.

Curtis takes a long pause before

responding. "Whatever you want," he says.

"Thank you." I take his hand. "Curtis, there's something I want to tell you."

"I think I already know. You don't want to return to Hollywood, do you?" There's a bittersweet smile on his face.

I shake my head and wrap my arms around my stomach. "I don't think I can. Too much has happened."

"So you're firing me, is that it?" There's no hint of criticism in his voice. "I'm kidding. I fully understand. I'll be here as your friend." He gives me a bittersweet smile. "Do you know what you want to do after this?"

"Yeah. As soon as Christa and I are discharged, we're going back home."

Curtis nods. A cloud of disappointment touches his features, but he quickly smiles to hide it from me. He's too slow, though. I know him too well, and it breaks my heart that I'm too broken to give him what he wants.

21

The pink and white cake is shaped like a baby bottle. It's so beautiful that I regret having to cut through it. But everyone is cheering me on.

A glow of warmth spreads through my chest as I look up to smile, then return my attention back to the cake. I watch as the silver knife with a pink ribbon on the handle sinks into the soft icing. I place the first slice on a clean paper plate.

"Take the first bite," Christa calls out over the excited giggles in the room.

The baby shower was a complete surprise. I was so focused on having a healthy pregnancy and writing my book that having a baby shower never crossed my mind. It wasn't even important to me.

In the months after the tragedy, I have hardly made contact with anyone, spending hours of my time inside my new cottage by the beach.

When we returned to Mistport, Christa and I sold the house we grew up in, both of us needing a new start. My priority was to create a beautiful new home for my baby.

Christa had met a wonderful man named Dennis—a psychologist—at our weekly group therapy sessions. After only a few weeks of dating, he proposed.

At first, I was nervous about her relationship, urging her to take her time first to get to know him. But she assured me he was the real thing. She also said that the cancer and the kidnapping had shown her that life is too short and can be taken away anytime. To calm my nerves, I had to remind myself that not every man is like Dax Pierce.

I gaze past the other faces in the room to find my sister's face. She looks so happy, happier than I have ever seen her before. Even though I don't have a man of my own, her happiness is contagious.

As I look around at the rest of my friends, some new and some old, I'm grateful. I cannot say I have reached the place where I'm truly happy, but I'm on my way.

The past seven months have been crazy with paparazzi chasing me everywhere, publishers approaching me with book deals, and producers with movie offers. Curtis was wonderful at keeping most of them off my back. Even though I don't pay him as my agent, he's still in my life as a friend, like we promised. We haven't seen each other since he came to see me at the hospital in Stonebay, but we speak on the phone from time to time. I don't call him as often as he says I should. I need the time to rediscover who I am.

Even though I didn't plan on it, writing my book has helped me heal in many ways. I have spent so many hours on it and now I'm almost finished.

Some people write books for years, but I'm desperate to get everything down on paper so I can move on. I'm still unsure what I'll do with it once I'm done. I know there will be publishers wanting to snatch it up, but I can't think about that right now. At the moment I'm writing it for me, not for the money. I'll decide what comes next after I write "the end".

Thankfully, I've earned enough in my short years of acting to have a small cushion to fall back on for a while. As Dax's wife, I had also been entitled to his assets, but I donated everything to the Obsession Inc. Organization that helps women in abusive relationships.

The one job I do a few times a week is volunteering at an abused women's shelter.

The rest of my time is spent reading on the beach, writing, and trying to get back to myself.

I stay away from reading the papers or watching the news when I can, because my story usually always pops up.

More details about Dax have emerged. Apparently, he had killed at least ten people, mostly women. The bodies of six of his female victims were found buried under the basement floor of the villa where I first discovered his dark side. A corpse was buried underneath the floor of each room, except two. I'm guessing one of the empty rooms was the one belonging to the Magnolia Girl since he had killed her outside the villa, in a faked suicide, and the other room was meant for me.

It sends a chill down my spine knowing that when he was showing me those rooms, he knew the corpses of those women were buried underneath.

I return my attention to my baby shower, amazed that people who once looked down on me are now showing me so much love and support. Even though I was distant emotionally, the moment I stepped foot back in Mistport, I was welcomed with open arms. It's ironic that I had run away in search of my freedom only to find it here in the end. This is my home, and these are my people. I feel safer here than in Los Angeles.

I lift my cake to my lips and bite into it, enjoying the sweet chocolate center. Christa comes to me and pulls me into a hug. The baby kicks between us. We both laugh.

"You look so beautiful pregnant," she says. "I can't wait to meet the little princess." She places both hands on my belly and the baby kicks again.

In a way, I was relieved when I found out the baby is a girl. I was afraid I would get a boy who resembles Dax. I feared he might grow up to be like his father.

Everyone gets some cake and we drink sparkling apple cider, but after two hours and too much excitement, I'm exhausted. While my guests continue partying out in the small garden outside, I relax on the couch, alone in my living room.

A feeling of contentment washes over me when I place my hands on my tummy and feel my baby moving.

I'm about to fall asleep, when Christa comes back into the house.

"There's someone at the door to see you."

I blink my sleepy eyes. "A late guest?"

"You can say that."

"Okay." I sit up straight. "Bring her in."

"It's a he."

"A man?"

"It's Curtis, sis."

My breath hitches. "What's he doing here?"

"Maybe you should ask him yourself."

"Okay." I'm still confused when Curtis walks into the room, but the moment our eyes meet, I realize what had been missing from my life, the last piece of the puzzle.

He's wearing blue jeans and a crisp, white shirt. "Hey. What. . ." I swallow hard. "What are you doing here?"

"A few weeks ago, your sister told me she was planning a baby shower for you. I know it's only for the ladies, but I hope you don't mind me showing up."

"No, of course not." I struggle to push myself to my feet. "It's good to see you." I hadn't realized until now how much I missed seeing him. Even though we haven't seen each other in months, it feels natural having him around.

"You don't need to do that. Sit, please." He comes to join me on the couch and pulls me into a hug I didn't know I missed. Then I pull back and gaze into his eyes. "Why did you come all this way? I have a feeling you're not here for the party. You missed all the fun anyway."

"Actually, I wanted to see you pregnant." He smiles, his eyes crinkling at the corners. "You are so beautiful." He raises a hand over my belly. "May I?"

"Yes," I whisper. My emotions are spinning out of control. I want to blame the hormones, but I know they aren't entirely at fault.

He lays a hand on my stomach. The baby does not kick this time, but the warmth from his palm radiates through my skin straight to my heart.

"Curtis, why are you really here?" His effect on me is more intense than I had allowed myself to believe. As I watch him, heat curls its way down my spine.

"Because there's no place for me in Hollywood, not anymore."

"You're quitting the movie business?"

He looks deep into my eyes and goosebumps form on my skin.

"Yeah, it's time. I think I had a good run." He lifts his hand from my stomach. "The thing is, after the Dax scandal of him stealing and killing his way into the movie industry, I realized there's so much dishonesty there, too many skeletons in many people's closets. It's not a place that brings me peace anymore."

I pluck at the hem of my skirt. "What do

you want to do with your life now?"

He leans back on the couch and stretches his legs out. "I'm thinking of buying a house someplace quiet and spending my life fishing. . . or something."

"Really?" I laugh. "I can't imagine you spending hours fishing. You'll be like a fish out of water."

"That's true." He rubs his chin. "Unless I have someone to do it with me."

I know where he's going and I don't stop him. I suddenly long to hear everything he has to say to me.

"Emma, I know you're in a different place in your life now, and you're not ready for more than friendship. I'm aware that the wounds are still fresh, but I also know that there's nobody I would rather be with."

"I'm pregnant, Curtis." I hesitate. "I'm pregnant with Dax's child. He will always be around me even when he's dead."

"That baby you're carrying is yours too. I can help you raise her to be a beautiful little girl and an amazing woman like you are."

"What are you saying?" I push a hand

through my layered pixie haircut.

He places a hand on my cheek. "Don't worry, I'm not asking you to marry me. . . yet." He gives me a mischievous grin. "Not unless you want to, of course."

Consumed by my emotions, I don't respond, so he continues.

"What I'm asking is your permission to be your neighbor."

"My neighbor?" My head snaps up. "What are you talking about?"

"I'm interested in the cottage next door. All I need to hear from you now is a maybe. Then one day when you're ready, I'll be here for more. I'll be next door." To my surprise, he pushes a hand into his pocket and comes out with a small jewelry box. "I bought this ring for you. You don't have to wear it now. But keep it until you know."

A smile creeps up on my face, warming my entire body. I reach for the box in his hand, but I don't open it, don't look at the ring. Not now. But I wrap my fingers around it and give him his answer. "Maybe," I whisper.

A lot will happen between now and

forever, many celebrations and many struggles, but when Curtis leans into me and presses his lips to mine, I know deep inside me that he's the man I'll one day come home to.

EPILOGUE

"Thank you for making me the happiest man in the world tonight." Curtis lifts a hand from the wheel and places it on my thigh.

I raise my left hand to admire my engagement ring, a simple diamond that means so much. "Thank you for not running away."

It's been two years since Curtis showed up at my baby shower with the promise to wait for me. As promised, he had given me the time I needed to heal. Even though we shared a kiss that day, it never happened again until the night Ella was born.

I had been so overwhelmed with joy from the experience of bringing my baby into the world with him holding my hand all the way, that when he congratulated me with a kiss, it felt right. He was the one. I had to go to hell and back to see that.

I gaze at the dark road ahead, thinking about everything that had happened after the kiss that confirmed our love for each other. The best part was watching my beautiful baby grow. She's so beautiful. Even though she has Dax's amber eyes, I see more of me in her.

Every time my mind takes me back there, back to the dungeon, I look at her and remember that beautiful things can be formed from broken things. *Broken Things* was the perfect title for my New York Times bestselling book. It just seemed fitting and honest.

I could never have anticipated the success of my self-published memoir. I was completely blown away when I woke up the morning after I hit publish to find it among the top 100 bestsellers. Since then, it went to top 10 and stayed there for weeks. Phone calls started coming in again from traditional publishers and movie producers promising to make me famous again. Each time, I politely declined their offers. I was honest with them. Fame had left a bitter taste in my mouth. I was not going back there.

"Are you happy?" Curtis gives me a brief glance.

"Right now, in this moment, I am."

"Well, I promise you many more moments like this."

"I can't wait." I press my hands to my flushed cheeks. "I look forward to forever."

Curtis parks the car in front of his cottage and we walk a few steps to mine, hand in hand.

We kiss on the porch underneath the yellow light from the lamp on the wall, then I unlock the door.

The lights are on downstairs, but Sadie, the babysitter, is nowhere to be seen.

"Maybe she fell asleep in Ella's room again. I'll go and check. Go to the bedroom. I'll join you soon."

On my way to Ella's room, I pull out the pins that had held up my updo. I love the feel of my shoulder-length hair falling free. I run my hand through it, appreciating the silky touch.

I drop the pins on a small table in the hallway. In front of my daughter's nursery, I stop to smile, then push open the door and freeze.

Ella is where she should be, sleeping soundly in her crib. I had expected Sadie to be sleeping in the armchair with a storybook on her lap, but she's not there. Someone else has taken her place.

A woman with stringy hair and black clothes is sitting where Sadie was supposed to be, watching my baby sleep.

"Who are you?" Fear showers my back like icy water. I reach for the nearest object that could be used as a weapon, a heavy album on the table nearest to the door.

The woman turns around and blood drains from my face. The face. The eyes. No, it cannot be. It's not her. It's not Dax's mother.

"I had to come and see her." Her eyes are sad, pleading.

I clutch the edge of the table for support. "You are. . . —you're—"

"I'm alive. He thought he killed me." She glances at her shaking hands. "He hit me on the head and threw me into the water. But God wanted me to live. I was barely conscious when I washed up on shore and someone found me."

"Get away from my baby." I tighten my hand around the album. "Get away or I'll call the police."

She nods and pulls herself up, but she's so weak, she sinks back down. "Sorry," she says with tears in her eyes. "The shock of everything my son did to you. . . to other people took a toll on my body."

"How did you get into my house?" I cross the room to stand between her and the crib, to shield my sleeping baby.

She drops her gaze to her shaking hands. "The babysitter. I told her the truth, that I'm Ella's grandmother. I said I would take care of her."

As relieved as I am that she, too, survived Dax's tortures, I'm shaken that she wormed her way into my house, into my life. What if I came home and she had taken the baby? The thought makes my stomach hurt. "I need you to leave."

"I will. Just. . . please let me look at her one more time." She tries to look past me at the crib, but I don't let her look at Ella.

"I said leave." I could call the cops on her, but something inside me won't let me. She may have survived the horrors of the Black Mamba, but there's no way she would survive long behind bars. She looks too weak and broken.

This time she manages to stand. As she takes a few steps toward the door, I notice that she's swaying.

She turns to look back at me. "Before Dax got rid of me, he asked me to put the pills—the abortion pills in your drinks. He told me what they were for. He wanted me to do his dirty work. I couldn't." Tears roll down her face as she leans against the wall. "I've made many mistakes in my life, but I couldn't kill my own grandchild. I flushed the pills down the toilet. I lied to him."

"Oh, my God," I say, sinking into the armchair. "You—"

"I didn't know if you would survive long enough to give birth, but I wanted to do something right for once."

"I had cramps. I was bleeding." I'm talking to myself instead of her.

"You were going through a lot of trauma. It's a miracle you didn't lose the child anyway."

Tense silence falls between us as I digest her words. Then I look up with tears in my eyes. "Thank you," I say. She scared the hell out of me by entering my house without permission and I don't know if I'll ever feel comfortable with her in my life, but she did save my baby. "What do you want?"

"Nothing more than this. I've spent months gathering the courage to come here. I was in town for two weeks." She shifts from one foot to the other. "I didn't think you would let me near her, so I waited for an opportunity to—"

"You were stalking us?"

"I'm sorry," she says. "I'm really sorry for everything. I hope one day you'll find it in your heart to forgive me."

I'm about to speak when Ella sighs in her sleep. I turn to look at her. She stirs but doesn't wake up.

"I won't bother you again. I'm going away."

I want to tell her to stay in our lives, to get to know her granddaughter, but the words are stuck in my throat.

"Where will you go?" I look back at her.

"To the bathroom first, if you don't mind."

I frown as I stand and show her to the one nearest Ella's room. I'm not so cruel that I would deny someone their right to use the bathroom.

I go back to kiss Ella on the forehead and close the door softly behind me.

I wait for Faith in the hallway. At the other end of the hallway, I can hear soft classical music playing in my bedroom. Curtis is waiting, but I have to deal with Dax's mother first. I'm still conflicted about what to do about her.

She stays too long in the bathroom, so I knock softly. She doesn't open the door. I wait a few more minutes and knock again. Nothing.

A cold feeling races down my spine. What is she up to in there?

When she still doesn't come out, I run to my bedroom. I have no choice but to tell Curtis what has happened as fast as I can get the words out.

His face is a mask of shock. He doesn't

even have a moment to process the information because I beg him to help me get into the bathroom. It takes a long time for him to knock the door down. When he finally does, it's too late.

Dax's mother is sprawled on the bathroom floor, her face white as a sheet. Curtis drops to his knees to feel for a pulse. He finds none.

A while later, the paramedics show up to confirm her death. Apparently, she had taken enough pills to overdose. Hours later, when I fetch Ella from her room, I find the note Faith left behind.

Dear Emma,

I'm sorry for the horrible things my son did to you. I will never forgive myself for not doing something sooner. I'll take my guilt to my grave. I just wanted to come and see that you and my grandchild are safe now. I wish I could stay to watch her grow into a beautiful woman. But I can't. I can't live with the memories anymore. I need some rest.

Goodbye, Emma. You will not see me again. Please protect my granddaughter from men like her father. When she's older, tell her I love her.

Faith

A few days after Faith's death, I take over the funeral arrangements—since she had no living relatives—and we bury her in Mistport, close enough so that one day, when my wounds heal more, I can take Ella to visit her grave.

Faith made many mistakes, but she was still Ella's grandmother, and she did the right thing in the end. She saved Ella's life.

With her death, a chapter of my life closed and I opened another. At her funeral, I made a conscious choice to look forward instead of behind me.

Unlike Faith, I choose life. I choose happiness. I choose Curtis. I choose love... real love.

THE END

Thank you for reading. If you enjoyed this book please consider writing a review, and recommend it to friends and family.

OTHER BOOKS BY DORI LAVELLE

Moments Series (4 books)
To Live Again Serial (3 books)
His Agenda Series (4 books)
Fatal Hearts Serial (3 Books)
Amour Toxique Serial (3 Books)
After Hours Series (4 Books)

For more information visit
www.dorilavelle.com

Printed in Great Britain
by Amazon